P9-CEZ-849

SNITCH

A NOVEL BY
VegasClarke

Life Changing Books in conjunction with Power Play Media
Published by Life Changing Books
P.O. Box 423 Brandywine, MD 20613

This novel is a work of fiction. Any references to real people, events, establishments, or locales are intended only to give the fiction a sense of reality and authenticity. Other names, characters, and incidents occurring in the work are either the product of the author's imagination or are used fictitiously, as are those fictionalized events and incidents that involve real persons. Any character that happens to share the name of a person who is an acquaintance of the author, past or present, is purely coincidental and is in no way intended to be an actual account involving that person.

Library of Congress Cataloging-in-Publication Data;

www.lifechangingbooks.net
13 Digit: 978-1934230763
10 Digit: 1934230766

Copyright © 2010

All rights reserved, including the rights to reproduce this book or portions thereof in any form whatsoever.

Acknowledgements
VegasClarke

First and foremost we like to thank God, who has given us the strength to overcome the worst and look to a brighter future.

To our publisher, Azarel, CEO of Life Changing Books, we sincerely thank you for making a dream a reality. You believed in us and took us under your wing. The support we received from you, Leslie and the rest of the LCB family was enormous. We look forward to working with you all in the future. Thank you and God bless.

To our beautiful Dior, you're our motivation and first born. We're so proud of you. We love you and couldn't have asked for a better daughter. Maverick, we love you because you are our "miracle" child. Mommy risked life to give you life and if it had to be done all over again, it would be. God watched over you and made you strong and is continuing to make you stronger. We love and cherish you both!

To our in-laws, we love you all and have come to be family and this goes for our friends as well.

To the Eighty81 Family- Kelton and Gabe, Ed (Duck), Jameel, and Dj Steph Floss, thanks for spreading our work and name through the city.

Shout out to Corey Spinks- I don't know who dances more, you or Clarke. Anges Adjaho, Lil' Marco from Youngstown, Clarence Voyant, Guillermo Jones, Omari, and

D'Amato Tyson. To Iyuana Nichole (Trophy Wife), Maurice & Lori Jones, Rondell & Antoinette Lewis. To Meia Jones, thanks for everything with "Keepin' the Faith Photography." To the Brigade, Next, and Martha's.

To all of the bookstores housing our book and giving us support, thank you! To all the urban fiction readers that support VegasClarke now and in the future, we sincerely thank you.

We hope that we got everyone and if we didn't, we sincerely apologize. We'll get you on the next go-round!

Much Love,
VegasClarke

Vegas

To my mother, Cheryl-I love you. Words cannot express how much I've learned from you. To my grandfather-Roland Morris. To my dad, Henry-Thanks for rolling with me when I didn't have anyone. To my Step-mom Kimberly Wilder-I really appreciate all the babysittin' you do for us and everything you do. Love you! To my Stepfather- DeWayne Jackson

To my one and only, Clarke-First off I would like to say, I know that I'm a difficult person to deal with at times, I appreciate your endurance with me. You have really worked hard on this project, and I'm so proud of you. I would like to thank you for giving me two beautiful children and being the strong woman I need in my life. I love you so much!

To my brothers, Brandon (Big B) Collier-Keep up the good work and never give up on your dreams. Marc Morris-Don't be afraid to follow your dreams. Andre Collier-Always remember that I believe in you and I support you in all of your endeavors. At the end of the day, I know you have my back when no one else does. Christopher Hobson-you my nigga and I love you nigga!

To my sisters, Charmen and Carmen (twins) - I don't have to say much because y'all know where y'all stand in my heart. Shannon-I know sometimes you think we're being hard on you, but we just want the best for you.

To all my cousins-Wesley & Christine, Steve, Laton, Milo, Lil Geoff, Koot, Jamere, Jackie, Warren, Jerry, Darren, Terrence (T-Dude)-thanks for rolling with me in Milan when the whole Ohio was against a nigga, CeCe, Mooch, Scum, Brint, Fallon, Dominique, Danielle, Billy Boy, Emmit, Nate & Will (twins)-from Valley, Gino Hinton and Anthony (Poosie) Wilkins.

To my niggas- Pedro, Qiana, Lauren (Lo) & Brooklyn, Clara, Tessa, Taccara, TK, Chal, Mel, Shawna-thanks for Starbucks and Cigars, Michael (Montay) Owens, Jermaine (Termite) Bennett, Kenneth (KB) Baker-my nigga who rode with me hard in Leavenworth whether right or wrong, Lil Griffin from St, Louis, Leeland (Amir) Muldrow, Mark (Nasir) Jenkins-from the NY that is preacher's son, Clifford (C-Murda) Square, Lil Red, Cuban Ant, Zeke, Ernest (Nu-Nu) Williams-no matter through thick and thin, one of da realest DC niggas I have ever met, Big Russ, Lazy Bone, Clayton, Germ, Jesse James from Illinois, William (Slow) Elzy, Bernard (B-Mac) Davis, Cid, Jared (Paper Boy)-Kansas City's finest, Darshawn (Darvic da Barber) Rorie, Spud-thanks for letting me chill in the salon! Marco, Big Baby, Samaj, Gup from Longwood, Tee Wee (Soo Woo), Tink from 30th, Rayvon, Mo-Dig, Daron, Big Ty, Woo, Ashley & Trail, Avant, Black Twan, Marvel Roach, Beverly Barnes, Tiffany from Shell, BG, Tommy Gunz from New York, Pete, Paul & Patrick from Valley, Big Dame, Larry from Main Street Deli, and Big Edmond Davis.

To Pimpin Knowledge from Flatbush, KC, Mick from Flatbush, Montana, Good Game, and Salahdeen (Sal)-Flyest nigga in the city.

A special thanks to Quentin Carter for hippin' me on to the writing game and exposing me to writing about the common issues in the urban community.

R.I.P-Grandma Sue, Mike Mike & Barry Joseph-real

niggas gettin' money from the start! Big Chest Barnes!

Shout out to my aunts, Patricia & Roz, love you. To my uncles-John, Junior, Charles, Mel, Tony, and Roland. Shout out to Abdul Salaam at "Under the Tree", West-side Chedda Boy-Brick, Jesse James-Joy Road., Ducko at the Joy of Music, and Jesus-Barber Caché.

Shout out to Louis (China Man) Valpais. Shout out and thanks to Mr. Nathaniel Gray for the positive encouragement. To the Weird Kid-stay focused on music, Meaty and Denario Smith, y'all too!

To all you hatin' ass niggas, suck it easy and swallow slow!

Clarke

I would like to thank my parents, Dale and Ronnell, who have always given me the support and means to do anything I ever wanted. You have made me a Black American Princess (BAP) to only strive for the finest things and be the best. You are the best parentals ever!

To my Vegas and best friend, we did this project as one and it was one of the best experiences in my life. I'm so very proud of you and I'll love you always.

To my sister Danelle, even though we don't see eye to eye all the time, I love you always, no matter what. You're always there when I need you!

To my little brother, Dale (D), I love having you as a little brother and we always have each other's back no matter what. Get your good grades and be someone positive in this world. No matter how old you get, you're always my little brother and I will always tell you what to do. I love you!

To my nieces Rylynn and Layla, you are some beautiful little girls and remember to always stay sweet. My nephew, Jaymon, you're so handsome and a handful, but I love you anyway! To my Goddaughter Leilani Chloe, you're beautiful and even though I don't see you often, you're always in my heart.

To my three wonderful grandmothers, Mary, Almira, and Katherine! I love you! To my Aunt Marilyn who I miss so much. RIP and I'll see you again. Your words of wisdom will stay with me forever. To my so cool Uncle Wilson, I love you and thanks for everything.

To my aunts-Beverly Johnson, Trenace Holland, Janice Johnson, Marzie Simmons, Yvonne Fernandez, and Heather Edwards. To my uncles- Jerome Johnson, Ronald Johnson, Kenneth Edwards, Sean Edwards, William (Boo) Edwards, R.I.P Monroe Johnson II & Daniel Johnson.

To my girls, you all came in my life at different times, but it was at the right times when you did. Much love! Rae-nala Brown, Jeri Ross Natale, Lady Shawn Axson, T'Pring (Muff) McKenzie, Carolyn (Nikki) Algee, Shanequa Niles, Tyra Coleman-Fowler, Sandra Marie Jackson, Nancy Jones, Diana Dior (LeShawn) Johnson, Stephanie Rowe, and Nat'e Gray, -Thanks for always checking up on me and never being fake and phony. You've accepted me for me and you're what I consider "pure" and genuine friends!

To my cousins who I love so much. We have all kicked it together, cooked together, argued together, cracked jokes together, and cried together. At the end of the day, we're family and we grew up tight. I love every last one of you guys. Monica Johnson, Monroe (Monty) Johnson III, Tamiko Johnson, Boohda Johnson, Tiffany Hardy, Joy Cleveland, Mikey Henderson, Tennille Henderson, Ronald (Lil Block) Johnson, Dandrelle Johnson, Cyrita Johnson, Chivonne Johnson, Jemar Johnson, Jayson Rogers, Tiarrah (Judy) Rogers, Johanna (Jojo) Rogers, Josh Rogers, Josiah Rogers, Jahiela Rogers, Laura Graves, Antoine Graves, Freddie Michelle Edwards, Brian Edwards, Shyvonne (Shoobee) Johnson, Shaundra Johnson, and Keenya (Kandy) Steele.

To all of my cousin's kids-it's so many and I can't name all of you, but I love you guys too. This should be a sign to stop having kids-thanks!

To my cousins Toni and Tee-Tee Bailey, y'all pre-ordered the first copies of SNITCH. Love y'all for that. Thanks for the support. To my cousins Tamera and Tiara Saddler, and Danielle Bailey, thanks for all the babysitting. Now that y'all are getting grown, no babysitting anymore? LOL! To my cousin Dana Johnson, I don't know why you haven't gone to "America's Next Top Model".

Shout out to Danielle Williams-thanks so much! Wayne and Lisa Carter, Darryl Miller, Ondrea Saffo, Sandra Blythewood-Hart, Sheree Smith, Tamala Magris, Tanyaa (Cookie) Roberts, Joe Marsh, and Karen Washington.

To Louisa Foster, I've known you since I was 15 years old and you and Unique have grown to be family. Besides this, you also give me the coldest weaves, Love ya!

Shout out to Makeeba at "Hair Café", you gave me the coldest mo-hawk! To Little Africa: Sedrick Craig, Jeff Johnson, Gino Del Rosso and Elliot Wade. To Donte (Ol' Skool) Jones, Reggie and Dane!

To all my family I didn't name because it is so many, I love you all anyway!

To the ones whom I thought were my friends and it wasn't genuine, it's fine now that I got the knife from my back, but it is what it is. Holla!

CHAPTER 1
2000

Hidden behind the tint of a black SUV, four masked men waited patiently for Shorty to call. Roscoe was the latest victim. He was getting a lot of paper on the Eastside of Cleveland, Ohio and was considered an old head at the age of thirty-five. He'd been selling dope for over a decade without getting busted by the police, or falling prey to the stick-up boys. Unfortunately for Roscoe, all that was about to change.

Drape sent Shorty at him, a red bone honey with a cute face, and dimples that gave off that innocent vibe. Shorty had long black tendrils that cascaded down her back and was Drape's gangster bitch who was down for whatever, whenever for him. It wasn't hard for Shorty to get close to any nigga Drape sicked her on. It could've been because she was slightly bowlegged and had one of those sexy, nasty types of walks with long legs, or the bad-ass body she possessed to go along with the walk.

On the other hand, Shorty was a lowdown dirty bitch, always following a dollar. If she thought a guy had money, she was on him hard until she got what she wanted. Most times, all it took was her infamous, mischievous smirk. Shorty was most definitely the worm on the hook for a baller. A hustler's downfall in the flesh.

Drape's cell phone rang. "What's da business?" he answered eagerly.

"He just dropped me off. Roscoe told me to call him at his house in twenty minutes, so he should be on his way," Shorty informed.

"Good lookin' baby. I'ma hit you tomorrow," Drape retorted before hanging up.

This was going to be the Scrilla Boys' last robbery lick. He paused deeply to think about how he, Tim, Tiger, and Romeo had formed their crew. Drape felt it was time they tried their hands in the dope game.

Drape, Romeo and Tim got out of the SUV, creeping into Roscoe's backyard to hide while Tiger stayed behind in the inconspicuous truck as a lookout. As they waited the twenty minutes for Roscoe to pull up, it seemed like eternity for the fearless goons. It was quiet and even though they'd ran the same scheme over a hundred times, a cloud of nervousness suddenly came about. It could never be determined what to expect from the victim.

Out of the blue, the sound of Roscoe's garage door startled Romeo as it began to rise. The bright lights of Roscoe's Range Rover reflected off the garage as he turned into the driveway. Roscoe tapped his garage door opener again, as he pulled inside the garage, then watched as it began to close. He sat in his truck momentarily gathering up the few items he had on the passenger seat, while Drape, Romeo and Tim quickly rolled under the garage door before it closed.

Within seconds the explosive sound of shattering glass echoed. Roscoe's heart thumped heavily when glass from the driver's side window suddenly burst onto him after being hit with the butt of Drape's pistol. Quickly, Drape reached through the window and grabbed Roscoe by the neck with his large python looking arms.

"Who in da muthafuckin' house nigga?" Drape demanded through clenched teeth as he held his pistol up to Roscoe's temple.

"Nobody!" Roscoe's voice trembled still shaken up from the surprise. Drape opened the driver's door slowly and yanked Roscoe out while still pressing the gun into his head. Once out the car and walking side by side, Drape's one hundred ninety-five pound chiseled body led Roscoe's narrow frame toward the door, which led into the house.

"Yo, Romeo, grab the keys!" Drape shouted.

Roscoe wasn't a praying man, but hoped like hell his little brother knew what to do since he hadn't stuck to their normal procedure. Roscoe's routine was to always blow his horn three times before entering the house. This code let his younger brother, Marc know it was him and that everything was okay. Roscoe's brother knew that if he did not hear the horn, he needed to hide quickly in the secret hiding place installed in the living room wall. Roscoe had been the only father figure in his brother's life ever since their parents died in a car wreck years ago but following in his footsteps was something he didn't want his brother to do. This was a strong motivation in Roscoe's hustle, but never thought it would actually come down to a robbery at gunpoint.

Romeo grabbed the keys out of the ignition and went straight for the door leading inside the house. Slightly bumping Drape with his muscular upper body he rushed past him quickly. Drape held Roscoe by the back of the collar, pushing him into the house, following Romeo and shoving the gun into his back as they walked.

"Where da money at nigga?" Drape griped as he came across Roscoe's face with his pistol, sending his small built body to the living room floor. Drape continued to pistol whip Roscoe until his face was covered with blood. Roscoe also continued to play stupid as Drape beat him repeatedly and demanded his stash.

"I got somethin' for dis muthafucka!" Tim muttered as he walked toward the kitchen. He came back out carrying a sharp butcher knife, and wearing a smirk.

"Hold yo' fuckin'' hand out," Tim demanded as he pressed a pressure point on Roscoe's arm forcing him to lay his hand flat on the living room table.

Drape nudged the barrel of his gun against the back of Roscoe's head. "Move muthafucka and I'm gone blow yo' fuckin' head off!" Drape yelled.

"Man, y'all ain't got to do this, I ain't got no paper," Roscoe pleaded.

"I'ma cut a finger off every time you stall. Matta fact let's start wit' dis finger right here. Da one wit' this big piece of bling on it," Tim uttered as he placed the sharp edge of the knife on top of Roscoe's pinky finger.

Marc peered fearfully at them through a small crack as the three masked men continued to torture his brother. At only eighteen years old, and in his senior year of high school, Marc was scared half to death. He knew he wanted to help his brother, but not only was Marc a lightweight, but Roscoe had always told him to save himself.

Marc was considered a square from the suburbs and didn't really know how to react in the situation. But when he saw Tim slide the knife across his own tongue this terrified Marc to the point of no return, especially when Tim licked the blood that dripped down his bottom lip.

Tim chopped the knife up and down on Roscoe's pinky finger and showed no remorse as it parted his flesh. Roscoe screamed in agony to the top of his lungs as his pinky finger was severed. Blood oozed from his finger and the white tissue was now exposed from under his skin. Tim chopped the knife one last time until the pinky finger fell on the table. Bone fragments flew in different directions and blood splattered everywhere, ending up on the white walls and Tim's pale, albino-looking skin.

"Here nigga, a souvenir," Tim joked as he tossed the

severed pinky finger to Drape with the huge diamond ring still on it.

Drape hopped back cringing at the sight of a stand alone finger on the table in front of him. However, he couldn't seem to take his eye away from the ring. "Damn, dat shit gotta be worth about 20k," he commented as Roscoe's platinum diamond glistened. For Drape it was like crack to a crackhead especially when he noticed that it looked like a VS1 to the naked eye. Drape loved jewelry and had to have the ring even if it meant taking it off the finger himself.

Suddenly, he reached closing his eyes and gagging at the mouth as he yanked the princess cut, three carat ring off Roscoe's finger. His boys laughed hard, except for Romeo who looked like he wanted to handle business.

"Just kill da nigga, Drape," Romeo complained.

Marc listened intently as Romeo said Drape's name. He played that name in his head over and over again hoping to never forget. He knew his brother would seek revenge.

Roscoe continued to be stubborn as Tim applied weight on his pressure point and began to repeat the same gruesome act on another finger. Marc couldn't take any more violence. He suddenly barged from behind the secret hiding place screaming.

"Leave him alone! Leave my brother aloneeeee!"

Tim's back was right in front of the secret hiding place door which caused Marc to charge him wildly from behind. Marc attempted to take hold of Tim, but the fear and anxiety prevented him from utilizing his tiny bit of muscle. Tim did a spin move and swiftly yoked him up, holding the knife up to his face. Tim immediately became enraged. A second later, Drape would've killed him.

"Don't kill him! I'ma tell y'all where the money at. Please… that's my brother. He don't have nothin' to do with this," Roscoe said begging for Marc's life.

"Where da paper at nigga?" Drape demanded as Roscoe stared in silence at the floor.

"Dat money worth more than yo' brother's life? Killem'," Drape continued.

Tim began to slide the razor sharp knife across Marc's cheek, slicing his flesh deeply. Blood instantly began to pour from the open wound. Roscoe shouted out his stash spot location as his brother cried profusely from the brutal pain with blood running from the fresh wound on his face.

Meanwhile, Romeo pulled back the large area rug that Roscoe had pointed to. His eyes lit up when he caught sight of the massive safe inside the wooden floor.

"Open it muthafucka!" Drape commanded.

Roscoe quickly crawled over to the safe and began punching in the combination. As soon as he punched in the last number, Drape opened the door and took out a hefty gym bag, tossing it to Romeo.

"Get it all," Tim instructed.

Romeo hit the chirp on his Nextel phone, "Pull out front," he ordered to Tiger.

"Since you did da right thing, I'm gone let yo' brotha live," Drape said. He then turned toward Roscoe, quickly pulling the trigger.

"Nooooooo!" Marc yelled as he watched Roscoe's body fall face first to the floor.

Tim loosened up his grip on Marc as he yanked away, running toward his brother's lifeless body. Drape, Tim, and Romeo ran out of the house and quickly hopped into the SUV where Tiger waited with a grin. Without delay, the Scrilla Boys sped off leaving Marc sobbing and cradling his dead brother's body.

SNITCH

The lick was successful just like Shorty told them it

SNITCH

would be. The pay; $750,000 cash. After splitting the money between them, Drape met Shorty back at her apartment duplex in the West Bank of the Flats.

"Drape, I don't appreciate gettin' the fuckin' crumbs. I put this whole thing together," Shorty whined counting her cut.

"Shorty, dat's right, all you did was put it together. You didn't do shit else. You lucky you got dat. I mean, thanks for the lick, but you gettin' ahead of yo'self."

"Whatever Drape, you always on some bullshit, but don't worry."

"What da fuck is dat suppose to mean? Shorty, don't play wit' me. I make sure you eat every damn time, $75,000 is a lot of dough."

"Drape, you got $225,000 all by yourself."

"Yeah, but I put in the real work. Im'a take $150,000 and cop some dope. That game gonna be gravy, and you gonna be with me."

"Okay, whatever Drape." Shorty huffed. *Your slick-ass always running game*, she thought to herself how payback was a bitch.

"You beginnin' to sound ungrateful. Let's not talk about dis shit again. Just open up your salon wit' your cut and be happy. Plus, you got da real estate thing goin' on so you should be straight." Drape paused. "My boys was happy wit' their $150,000 a piece. They gone cop some dope and come up in the game wit' me. So you do the same. Be happy and shut the fuck up."

Shorty ignored Drape but refused to let him play her while his "pampered" bitch, Diona got to live in the lap of luxury. She wanted to be angry but could never fight off the fact that she loved everything about Drape; the way he pimped when he walked, the way he talked grimey and dressed thuggish. She knew it wasn't the fact that he was half-

black, half-Puerto-Rican that had her feeling horny. She pre-
ferred deep, pitched black men resembling charcoal, contrary
to Drape's mocha colored skin.

"Fuck it, Drape," she finally uttered, but knew he
would pay one way or another. "You win. I'm not gonna
waste time being mad at you. Just give me some dick, nigga."

CHAPTER 2
2003
(THREE YEARS LATER)

Drape sat slouched in the chair on his mother's front stoop counting stacks of money and talking to his brother Angel. Angel with his high-yellow skin tone and patchy skin was the exact opposite of Drape other than the fact that they both had good hair. It was evident that they had different fathers, yet no one could ever tell considering their close relationship.

They both waited patiently for the rest of the Scrilla Boys to arrive. They could hear Nelly's *"Air Force One's"* flooding the Mark Levinson sound system in Tiger's red corvette as it cruised up the street toward the house. The wide streets in the suburb of Lakewood, Ohio where Drape's mother lived left room for the sun to shine, reflecting off Tiger's fresh paint job.

"Drape, tell that nigga don't pull all up on my bumper," Angel demanded.

"Nigga, ain't nobody gonna hit yo' shit," Drape said motioning for Tiger to stop as he pulled in the yard.

Angel didn't want him to get close to his 1971 candy apple green Chevrolet Chevelle, which sat on twenty-two inch Dalvins spinner rims.

"Damn boy, you really protective over that big piece of

steel you got over there!" Tiger joked as he got out of his car wobbling like he owned all of Cleveland. His Chinese symbol medallion, which symbolized money, glistened with an array of colors in every baguette and rested on his over-sized upper body.

.   "What up nigga?" Drape said giving Tiger dap.

"Shit," Tiger replied. "Just hungry, nigga." He rubbed his hand across his low cut fade and freshly lined goatee.

Drape laughed.

All three men stood outside in the driveway talking as Romeo, and Tim pulled their new cars on the street and hopped out like they were on time for something big. Everyone began walking toward the house.

Drape and Angel's mom, Patty greeted the boys walking through the front door.

"Hey y'all!" Patty said.

"How you doin, Mama Patty?" Tiger replied.

"I'm fine baby," she said giving him a hug. "How's your Mama?"

"She good," Tiger responded.

"Hey Mama Patty!" Tim sang in jealousy.

"Come here and give me a hug!" Patty responded, giving more hugs than necessary.

"Don't forget about me, Mama Patty!" Romeo commented.

"Boy, ain't nobody forgot about you, come here. You look just like you did as a kid," she commented as she slid her hand across his smooth, bald head. "Still cute as a button." She smiled. "You still got all the girls chasing you?" she asked, already knowing the answer.

"Naw. Not really." Romeo blushed.

"All my boys are here. Just like old times." She smiled again. "I got some greens, macaroni & cheese, and baked chicken in the oven. I'll fix y'all some plates when it's ready,"

Patty announced.

"Thanks Ma, we'll be downstairs," Drape replied.

"Hey Drape," his mother called out to him. "You're keeping your eye on your brother, right?"

"Of course Ma. Why you ask dat?"

"I just worry about him so much. You know, he's not rough like you. Sorta needs a little guidance ….never having his father around and all."

Drape frowned a little. "My father was never around too much either."

"I know, but you're strong willed…can pull through anything. I don't know what I would do if anything ever happened to either one of you."

"I got dis Ma," he boasted. "I'll take care of Angel." He winked at his mother letting her know that he loved Angel just as much as she did. Surely he wouldn't let anything happen to his baby brother.

All the boys went downstairs to the basement so they could discuss business until the food was ready. After a couple shots of Remy VSOP, Drape reached behind the bar and pulled out a large duffle bag. The bag contained 15 kilos of cocaine.

"Damn, dis nigga is chargin' us too much for dis shit. We need to get a new connect," Drape announced. "We makin' a killin' off dis shit."

Drape unzipped the large duffle bag and dispersed the fifteen kilos of cocaine between him and the Scrilla Boys. He stopped, opened one of the bags, and dipped his pinky finger into the white powder allowing a small portion to rest inside his nail.

"Damn, why you gotta be puttin' a hex on us wit' Roscoe's ring," Romeo announced. "Turn that bling the other way."

"Nigga, I told you over a year ago, dis my ring," Drape boasted while sampling the product.

"Damn, I'm ready to get me some money!" Angel broadcasted, while rubbing his hands together swiftly.

Drape shot him a look that told him to back off. "Don't I look out for you enough? You got you a nice old school and I keep you with a couple dollars in yo' pocket, man. Plus, you got a good girl and a daughter. When I get my shit to where I want it to be, I'ma set you up wit' a nice business so you can be the man you need to be for yo' family. You don't need dis shit in yo' life, trust me, dawg. Too much come wit' dis, lil' bro'," Drape preached. "It's either jail or a burial."

"Yeah, fall yo' young ass back," Tiger commented after giving Angel a sharp smirk. "You too young, dawg."

"And you too fat, nigga," Angel blasted while looking at his Triple X t-shirt. "Besides, nigga, you're not that much older than me. I'll be twenty in a couple of months." Angel gave off a sarcastic look. "I'm only three years younger than all y'all niggas, with the exception of Tim's old ass."

"Whoa…whoa," Tim commented. "I'm wise, nigga," he joked knowing that he was only twenty-five.

"Besides, I don't wanna hear that shit. Y'all nigga's making big money, so be easy," Angel shot back as he walked up the stairs.

Patty walked to the top of the stairs and shouted, "The food is ready!"

Like a hungry pack of wolves, Drape and his boys scurried upstairs to get their plates. After demolishing their hearty meals and making plans to meet at *Christie's Gentlemen's Club* an hour later, they each grabbed their three kilos of cocaine a piece.

"Bye, Mama Patty," they said simultaneously leaving out the door.

"Tiger, tell your mother I said call me!" she yelled as they all walked toward their cars.

For Drape, it was good seeing all his childhood friends

getting money and seeing them all together. The streets were cruddy and sometimes came with a cost, so to know that they were all okay and had each other's back made him feel good. He just needed to keep Angel out of the game.

SNITCH

The Scrilla Boys entered *Christie's Gentlemen's Club* looking like stars. They all decided to wear their iced out "SB" medallions hanging from their platinum chains. Each piece of jewelry had a hefty price tag of $65,000. Drape walked up to the bouncer and gave him dap. The bouncer did the same with the rest of the crew. The manager on duty walked up shortly after.

"What's up Drape?" the manager said in his Russian accent.

"Shit, we tryin' to make it rain in here. We need a private table wit' five bottles of Cristal' and a bottle of Remy VSOP. Also, send over a couple of da baddest bitches in da club," Drape instructed.

"Okay, make yourself comfortable and the barmaid will be right over with your bottles," the manager replied.

"Thanks." Drape peeled a $100 dollar tip off his thick wad of bills and handed it to the manger before walking inside with his entourage right behind him.

"It's some fine bitches in here!" Romeo announced.

"We bout to make it rain on these hoes!" Tiger joked, pumping his huge fist in the air.

"Oh yeah…how much paper you bring up in here?" Romeo asked trying to shit on Tiger.

"Enough. You know how I do," Tiger shot back. He rubbed his large stomach signaling a food order.

The manager did what he said and sent everything Drape requested. Before long each Scrilla Boy guzzled down the liquor as if it were water and was soon fucked up. Drape took a seat a few feet away, peeping the scene. He watched as Tiger and Romeo got lap dances from several of the strippers then threw hundreds on the floor for the ladies to get once they were done with their kinky shows. Kelis' *Milkshake* pounded through the speakers as Drape sat confidently in the chair with his jewels on blast. He thought about the sexy women and how some of them couldn't dance. He knew he could have any bitch in the club. But for Drape, the chase was better than the catch.

Drape took a swig from his bottle of Cristal and watched closely as a white chick walked up to Tim. She had on a ton of make-up with long brown hair. She was more than conceited with big succulent breasts, and wasn't Tim's type.

"Hey baby, you want a dance?" the girl asked.

"No, sweetheart, I'm good. I don't like gettin' lap dances."

"What, you don't want to pay for it or something?" she shot back with attitude.

"Nah, I just don't like a funky pussy rubbin' up against me, fuckin' up my clothes," Tim replied sarcastically, then pretended to iron out his expensive-looking jeans with his hands.

"Fuck you then!" the girl screamed.

"Bitch, get da fuck out my face! How about you let one of my niggas put some real money in yo' pocket, "Tim said going into his pocket and throwing a penny at the girl. "You only worth dis penny hoe!"

Romeo and Tiger rushed over to see what the commotion was all about. Together, they started hurling insults at the girl, throwing dollars at her. Her face was bright red with embarrassment.

"Tim what's goin' on?" Drape asked, coming over to where he was.

"Dis hoe talkin' reckless out her mouth. She mad 'cause I ain't want no lap dance from her, nasty ass!" Tim responded.

"Shut the fuck up!" the girl spat back.

"You shut the fuck up bitch!" Tim responded. "I spend too much muthafuckin' money in dis' club to deal wit' these types of hoes. We out!" Tim griped.

Tim didn't want to be there any longer, he motioned for the Russian manager to come over. He left $3,000 to cover the bill, which was pennies to him then walked out with the Scrilla Boys close behind. *A night ruined because of one dumb hoe,* Tim thought to himself. He knew he didn't have to flip out like that and ruin things for his crew. But it was all for one; and one for all. Besides, the liquor had gotten the best of him. They were all outside walking to their cars and walked up on Drape's 500SL Mercedes Benz first.

"You good Drape?" Tim asked.

"I'm good. Nigga, are you good?" When Tim nodded his head, Drape gave him a pound. "I'm out," he responded, slurring his words slightly. "My lady keeps callin' me."

Tim laughed. "Damn man, Diona still stalkin' you?"

"Yeah man, hit me tomorrow. Be safe!" Drape said driving off.

He chuckled to himself thinking about how crazy his long-time friends were and how he was tired of the dumb chicks that laced the club. He wanted to go home to peace and pussy, but knew he'd have to argue first about being out with his boys. *It was always about making a dollar,* he thought as he pulled off.

SNITCH

CHAPTER 3

It was one of those wet gloomy days when you just laid up with your girl, cuddling, and watching movie after movie. That's just what Drape was doing, but would've rather been out chasing money and possibly a bitch or two. It was the spirit of a hustler. His connect hadn't had any work for the past couple weeks. Consequently, Drape sold his last bit of drug supply a couple of days ago. Diona was his heart, so cuddling with her wasn't so bad, plus he'd promised her he would spend the day with her in the comfort of their posh home.

Diona had the perfect house fit for a BAP...Black American Princess. Drape didn't spare any expense where Diona was concerned. They lived in Moreland Hills, a suburb of Cleveland, Ohio. Their 4,388 square foot, five bedroom home sat on a secluded 2.8 acre wooden lot. The home was immaculate with all the trimmings including a two-story stone fireplace and private decks. The pristine beam and vaulted ceilings added a classic touch within the property. It also encompassed walls of glass throughout the house. Diona loved her home and Drape wanted to make Diona comfortable since she was often alone.

Drape looked at Diona intently as he grew impatient. He couldn't bear sitting in the same place for a long period. He and Diona lay cuddled on their soft pillow top mattress, which sat high on their hand-carved finished mahogany four-post king size bed. She laid with her arm nestled between his armpit. Happy spending time with him, Diona's cheek rested on his chest where she felt most comfortable. They'd been arguing a lot lately, especially with Diona being hormonal and approaching twenty-six weeks. She believed he put her and their unborn child on the back burner for his hustle. She didn't understand that in order for her to have the house, all the minks, jewelry, and money he gave her, Drape had to hustle hard and even harder to keep climbing the ladder in the dope game. Everyone knew maintaining in the dope game was just barely surviving.

Drape's cell phone constantly rang as they rested, but he pretended as if the ringing didn't exist. Reaching for his cell phone in front of Diona was like reaching for a gun in front of the police. Desperate to see what he was missing, he leaned over and grabbed the cell. Diona cut her eyes in disgust.

"Who dis?" he asked the unknown caller.

"Sheen nigga, damn! I need you to swing by."

"Bet. Gimme an hour," Drape replied angrily.

Diona sucked her teeth, raised her freshly arched eyebrows, and jerked her head back while staring at him angrily.

"Nigga, you ain't shit," she mumbled as Drape and Sheen finished their conversation. "Damn, I see your word not good when it comes to me. Let one of those bitch ass niggas call you and you hop up quick. I want you to spend more time at home. You spent more time with me when you were robbing muthafuckas!" Diona barked reverting back to her proper voice.

"I ain't in the fuckin' mood to be arguin' wit' you. You ain't complainin' when a nigga buyin' 'dem Louis Vuitton's and icin' yo' ears and shit, or takin' yo' spoiled ass on shoppin' sprees. Dat shit cost money and dis is how I get it. Money don't grow on fuckin' trees," Drape shot back.

SNITCH

"Let's not get it twisted, Drape, I was spoiled before you, so save that Nino Brown speech for someone who actually believes your stupid ass. Remember, I'm with you because I love you, not for all that materialistic shit. Talk that shit to a bitch who doesn't have anything. Life is more than what you seem to think. I hope you wake up one day and see that," Diona snapped as she threw a Deer Park water bottle at the back of his head.

Drape flinched, looking at her like she was crazy for throwing the bottle. He didn't even respond back to her because he knew she was telling the truth. But the streets were his life and he wanted to continue to give her a life she was accustomed to. This was the only way he knew to do it.

Drape walked toward the living room as he dialed Peanut. Paintings by Jean Michael Basquiat garnished their walls in the living room of bold-expressionist art. This was one of Diona's favorite African-American artists, and seemed as though his work glared at Drape as he talked on the phone.

Peanut was his back-up connect when his primary connect didn't have any work. He and Peanut beat around the bush for about five minutes before he told Drape to stop by. Diona followed him into the living room still wanting to express herself. Drape turned around facing Diona and began stroking her stomach with his left hand. He then kissed her on her lips and began rubbing her swollen pussy with his right hand.

She began to moan. "No, you pissed me off," she panted.

"I love you Diona," Drape said ignoring her.

He pulled her down on their oversized Italian leather couch and opened her legs wide so that every bit of her pussy was in his face. Quickly, he yanked her moist La Perla thong to the side and dove inside, making crazy love to her clit. As Diona became more excited, Drape worked his tongue in and out…around and around…like and artist shaping a sculpture, stopping between slurps to tell Diona how much he loved her.

Luckily, Diona's moans drowned out the sounds of Drape's cell phone constantly ringing. But nothing mattered to Diona anymore- nothing but Drape's firm hands gripping her ass and sucking her juices completely from her body. Soon, Diona began to pant…so hard that she'd lost her breath for what seemed like seconds.

"Oh my God! Drape!" She grabbed the waves on the back of his head.

Drape held her legs down firmly, almost fighting as Diona's body started to shake with convulsions. But that wasn't enough. Diona needed to know that she was still his number one. Drape's tongue dove deeper and deeper….and he continued to lick, until Diona exploded her sweet juices into his mouth.

Within seconds, like a horny jackrabbit, Diona ascended her fat swollen pussy onto Drape's love stick ready to take all. She pounced up and down with pleasure as her ass jiggled and her big bubbly eyes rolled to the back of her head. Drape uncontrollably grabbed her apple bottom with both hands, feeling how juicy her booty was.

"Ahh, shit!" he screamed.

"Ohh baby, I'm about to cum!" Diona gasped in between groans.

Diona continued to bounce her ass up and down on his pole until he exploded into her honey canal. As shivers jilted through her spine, it wasn't long before she fell onto her man's chest. Drape was glad he'd pleased her and wanted Diona to know that he loved her. More importantly, he wanted her to chill and quit bugging out. He and Diona hopped in the shower where he washed her from head to toe. The square shower head, mounted in the ceiling cascaded over both of their bodies while Diona got pampered. Drape admired her body as he bathed her natural beauty. She was mocha-colored with thick long hair, which fell a couple inches past her shoulders. Her skin was smooth and silky, which showcased no blemishes or signs of a hard life. However, what Drape loved the most was her thick thighs and a fat ass that adorned her backside. Drape had always craved her, but being pregnant made her look even more radiant and sexy. He hated to tell her that he had to leave, but he knew he had to take care of his business.

"Diona, ride wit' me to run some errands," he suggested.

"I don't know."

"Come on. It won't take long," Drape replied.

"Okay I'll go, but I don't want this to be all day. I'm hungry too."

"We'll get you somethin' to eat. Now, let's get ready," Drape said. He was about to walk away when he looked back at his girl. "Baby, I love you!"

"I love you too, Drape."

Thirty minutes passed before Diona threw on a Bebe jogging suit with a fitted tank top underneath, showcasing her protruding belly. Her hair was pulled back into a sleek ponytail showing off her one karat princess cut diamond earrings. After hearing Drape say to meet him downstairs in five, she rushed to apply a thin layer of Mac lip gloss across her sexy plump lips while Drape slipped on a pair of butter wheat Tims to go with his Seven jeans, white t-shirt, and an Indians baseball cap.

Drape grabbed the money he was going to use to pay Peanut and put it into a Nike shoebox.Once outside, the couple walked hand- in-hand out to Diona's Escalade where Drape placed the shoebox in the trunk before driving off.

By the time Drape pulled up to Peanut's crib, he was perched on his front porch steps, looking thirsty as a white mouth mule. He rose up with his pants hanging below his waistline and began to approach their truck as they pulled into his driveway. When Drape got out the car, Peanut waved, but Diona rolled her eyes with a condescending attitude.

"Yo' whas'sup? What's the deal son?" Peanut grumbled in his deep New York accent as he extended his hand out to Drape. "She mad as a bitch, huh?" Peanut continued.

"Yeah, I know." Drape grasped his hand and pulled him in close. "So, what you want fo' a brick?" Drape asked stepping away from Peanut.

"$20,000."

"Damn, dat's high!" Drape protested as he rubbed his chin.

Drape and Peanut has been through the same scenario many times before. Peanut knew that no matter what price he shot at Drape, he was going to cop. It was no secret that Drape only came to him when his connect didn't have anything. $20,000 wasn't that high, but it was six grand extra than what Drape normally paid with his connect. He couldn't and wouldn't knock Peanut's hustle. He was still going to make a killing after he cooked it up.

"Fuck it, let me get two," Drape said then pivoted toward the truck. He popped the trunk and pulled out the shoebox with fifty grand inside of it. He peeled $10,000 off of it and stuffed it deep into his pocket. He then handed Peanut the box.

"Yo' son, give me an hour. I gotta go get it," Peanut said walking toward his car.

"Don't take all fuckin' day," Drape said, letting him know he was pressed for time. He then hopped back in the truck with Diona.

"He'll be right back," Drape said as he laid his seat back and shut his eyes.

Diona had an attitude not only because she didn't want

to wait, but the fact that Drape's phone kept ringing wasn't helping either. She was grouchy and agitated, but laid back to relax as Drape began talking to her in a soft tone. An hour passed quickly after Peanut left, yet it seemed to serve as well needed time between Diona and Drape. The two shared thoughts about the baby and her future. She would be graduating from Cleveland State University in a few months and would have a Bachelors Degree in Psychology and minor in Political Science. Her goal was to obtain a Doctorate Degree in Psychology and become a licensed psychologist.

Drape on the other hand told Diona he wanted to get out the streets but didn't know how. He always felt he had dreams, but his fears got in the way. Crazy as it sounded Drape wanted an exclusive Day Spa for Men. One with a membership; fifteen hundred a month. It would be some sorta Secret Society where hair cuts were on the house, and men where serviced by chicks in thongs.

Diona began looking at her man sideways. "Why the fuck did I decide to have a baby by you?" She rolled her eyes hard.

Drape rubbed her shoulders playfully. "'Cause you wanted yo' baby to have good hair like me."

"You really believe that don't you?"

Peanut's knocking on the truck window and the ringing of Drape's phone startled them, interrupting their conversation. Drape stepped out of the car. He rose on the tip of his toes with his arms extended over his head as he let out a yawn.

"Nut you on some bullshit," Drape complained and followed Peanut over to his car.

"I know son, my fault. Yo' I counted the money, and that shit was two g's short," Peanut commented.

"Two g's short, that's some bullshit. I counted each stack twice," Drape said with an attitude.

Peanut quickly got defensive. "Yo' son I ain't gotta beat you out of no petty ass two g's."

It wasn't the fact Peanut said the money was short that really got Drape upset, although it played a major part. It was the fact he was taking so long to get back to Diona. He was already walking on eggshells with her. Plus, he had his licks waiting. Drape pouted as he reached in his pocket and pulled out the ten grand. He peeled off another two grand and gave it to Peanut. Drape then leaned into Peanut's driver side window and grabbed the two bricks off the seat concealed in a book bag. Drape was pissed off and got back inside the car where his phone was impatiently waiting. His cell phone hadn't toned down a bit since they left the house. As Drape drove to his secret apartment where he cooked the dope, he got angrier at the thought of Peanut accusing him of being short. Even though two grand was nothing, he knew Peanut had beat him out of some money. If it wasn't for Shorty being a close friend to Peanut, he would've stuck him up a long time ago. Peanut was known for always pulling some slick shit.

Soon, he and Diona arrived at his cook-up apartment and sped inside. Drape always told Diona that the apartment belonged to a friend who he let him use it to do his thing occasionally. The apartment was used only for cooking dope and from time to time, fucking a trustworthy broad. It was furnished from head to toe with leather couches and plasma TV's in every room. The only person who had access to the apartment was Drape and Shorty. As soon as they entered the apartment, Drape rushed into the kitchen, cutting the stove on and taking out his cooking utensils. He had a lot to get done in a short amount of time.

"Damn, are you in a hurry," Diona complained as she closed the door behind her.

"I got shit dat need to be done," Drape snapped, as he began breaking down one of the bricks. He put his cell phone on silent and placed it on the counter. He was tired of the constant ringing. *Besides, I know it's that nigga Sheen and I'm not ready yet.*

"Baby I'm hungry," Diona whined as she came up behind him.

"Mami' go get you sumthin' to eat," he suggested. "Daddy gotta work."

Drape was a chemist in the kitchen when it came to cooking dope. He could blow a thousand grams to eighteen hundred with just a hundred and fifty grams of baking soda and little water.

"Here," Drape said as he handed Diona the keys to her truck. He still needed to breakdown the dope, so leaving with her wasn't an option.

"You want something?" she asked.

Draped shook his head. "No, I got all I need right here."

"I'll be right back," she replied as she grabbed her Gucci purse off the counter, and then walked out the door.

Twenty minutes passed as Diona walked back through the door carrying a McDonald's bag and chomping down on some fries. Before she could get her feet inside his cell phone started as soon as he took it off silent. "Here we go," she said, sitting on the couch.

"Damn Sheen, give me a break. I'm comin' nigga," Drape said to himself. This was motivation for him to continue moving swiftly, staying on track.

Ten minutes later, Drape was pushing Diona back out the door then rushed her to the truck. He'd finished cooking his dope in record time and was ready to hit off his licks who were waiting on him. Once again, the phone rang. However, this time Drape finally answered.

"Where da fuck you at?" Sheen shouted impatiently in the phone.

"I should be there in bout ten minutes. No bullshit, I know I told you an hour ago. Just sit tight for ten minutes." Drape spattered out the lot after hearing the aggravation in Sheen's voice.

-CLICK-

When they arrived at Sheen's house, he was about to pull out of the driveway. Trying not to lose a sale, Drape sped up behind him, grabbed the package that was sitting in between the console and jumped out.

"Dawg, you been spinning a nigga so long, I was about to go holla at somebody else," Sheen said as Drape followed behind him and toward his front door.

"Have I ever told you I was comin' and didn't come? You an impatient ass nigga," Drape spat.

"Whassup wit' Shorty? Tell her I said if a nigga don't come up to her shop, a nigga don't hear from her. Tell her I said since she opened up da shop and got dat new whip, she done changed on a nigga," Sheen announced. Shorty and Sheen had been close friends since high school. She was the one who'd plugged him with Drape.

"Shorty just being Shorty," Drape replied as he and Sheen walked through the front door and up the hallway stairs.

Diona gazed at Drape from the car as he and Sheen strolled through the front door. Just looking at him made her pussy wet. She lustfully watched his tall, sexy body strut like he owned the world. She loved the fact that he was super confident when he conducted business, and was especially feeling his low-cut ceaser.

Diona loved him so much she hated him. All of her friends said she was in love with the dick, but that couldn't be any further from the truth. Deep down, she knew he loved her unconditionally, no matter what and her love for him was just as strong. She speculated about him and different women, but she knew he wouldn't risk losing her for them. Her parents couldn't understand how a soon to be college graduate such as herself, had gotten involved with a street thug who didn't seem to want anything better in life. Diona came from a good background with her father being a prominent defense attorney and her mom, a psychologist, both with their own practices. Upon graduation, Diona was set to work with her mom and then take over her practice, once she received her Ph.D.

Drape quickly handled his business with Sheen and hurried back to the truck. He was smiling from ear to ear as he approached the vehicle, relieved to have straightened out the business with Sheen's nagging ass. He opened the door to the Escalade and got in, tossing a bag of money onto Diona's lap, then placing the rest of the package in the compartment between the driver and passenger seats.

"Put dat on da floor," he said pointing to the money. "Dats ten grand," he told her pulling off. Drape smiled at what he'd accomplished in such a short amount of time.

"Here, your phone was ringing *again* while you were in there," Diona said handing him the cell.

He looked at the screen, "Yo' nosey ass had to look at da numbers in it, huh."

"You damn right," Diona shot back. "Tim called too. I told him to stop stalking you, and that you were supposed to be spending time with me and not them for once."

Drape simply shook his head. As he was about to respond, his cell rang yet again. "Who dis?" he answered not noticing the number.

"Malik, I didn't know a hour meant five hours nigga."

"Man, I forgot all about yo' ass. You lucky I was on my way back home. Don't go nowhere, I'ma be pullin' up in fifteen minutes."

Drape hung up noticing Diona looking at him sideways. As bad as he wanted to go home so they could finish cuddling, Malik was the one that he couldn't refuse. He and Malik had become close while in prison after Malik observed three racists crackers and Drape in a knock-down scuffle. In Drape's defense, Malik pulled out a shank and stabbed one of the dudes like it was nothing; ever since, he and Drape had a bond. At the time, Drape was serving a three month sentence for a probation violation and was being released the following week. He promised Malik who was coming home a month later that once he got out, he would put him on the team.

While Drape drove to Malik's crib, he noticed Diona's body language as she leaned against the door, gazing out of the window in complete silence.

"What's wrong, Babe?"

"Forget it Drape," Diona spat.

"Dis it, I swear. After dis we goin' back home, I promise," he said apologetically.

"I don't believe shit you say," Diona sulked.

Drape honked the horn as he pulled out in front of Malik's crib and parked cattycornered. He grabbed the package from in between the console as he opened the door in a hurry. Malik stood in the doorway holding the door open as he approached.

"What's up dawg?" Drape greeted his boy with a bump of the shoulder. "Hey, whassup Tina?" Drape spoke to Malik's girlfriend who sat on the couch with her cousin Dee Dee in between her legs braiding her hair.

"Heeeey Drape!" they sang in a flirtatious way.

"Dee Dee, I thought you were gonna have dem clothes for me last week?" Drape asked.

"Boy I had dem damn clothes fo' a week sittin' in that damn corner." She pointed. Everyone in the hood knew she was a professional booster.

"C'mon dawg!" Malik interrupted. He stood by his bedroom door kicking clothes out the way as Drape approached the junky room. "Here," he said attempting to hand Drape the five thousand dollars he owed him.

"Hold up," Drape insisted, kicking the remainder of the clothes away as he shut the door. Drape pulled a half of key out of the bag he was carrying and gave it to him. Malik then handed Drape the money as he grabbed the half of key.

"You owe me $13,500. I'ma call you in a week," Drape uttered as he placed the 5k in his top shirt pocket. "Damn, I left my phone in the car," he said out loud, "have my money next week," he ended before walking out the room.

One thing about Drape was that he didn't mind giving dope on credit, especially when it was stepped on. He grabbed the bag of clothes that Dee Dee had copped for him on his way out of Malik's front door.

"Good lookin' Dee Dee," he said making his way down the hallway steps and back outside to the truck. Once he was outside, Drape noticed how furious Diona was.

"Don't ever leave me in the car that damn long by myself!" Diona fussed as Drape hopped inside. "I'm six months pregnant, remember? I should've kept my ass at home," she badgered as her head bobbled about. "You call this spending time?"

"I'm sorry baby. Take dis money and add it wit' da rest. It should be twenty three thousand total."

Drape placed the package with the drugs back into its previous location and tossed the huge Gap bag in the backseat. Diona immediately grabbed the bag and opened it. Her attitude had left just that fast as she rambled through all of the baby clothes in the bag. The bag contained a mixture of Polo, Baby-Gap, a few items from SaksKids, and two pairs of Gucci booties. It was stuffed to capacity.

"Aweeeee, Drape…you were thinking about our baby?"

Diona's attitude came back when Drape's phone rang and she noticed Shorty's name appear on the caller ID. Diona started to feel nauseous. The thought of that grimy bitch, Shorty made her skin crawl.

"Take me home Drape!"

CHAPTER 4

Drape drove off from Malik's thinking about how much money he'd made for the day and how The Scrilla Boys had come so far from the little kids of the projects. They were making so much money that they were officially hood rich. It appeared that nothing could get in the way. While both Drape and Diona were in deep thought and three blocks away from Malik's crib, Drape noticed an ambulance, two police cars with speedily flashing lights, and sirens screaming in his rear view mirror. They were approaching hastily from behind. Like every other car on the road, he pulled over to let them pass.

Suddenly, the ambulance's tires screeched as it cut in front of the Escalade and slammed on the brakes. The rear doors suddenly swung open and two plain-clothes detectives jumped out with their guns drawn. Drape's heart rate increased drastically and his jaw dropped.

"Put the car in park and stick your hands out the window slowly! Toss the keys out," another detective demanded.

Drape peered in his rear view at the two police cars behind him that prevented him from going in reverse. Diona screamed to the top of her lungs. She was hysterical as she held onto her plump belly. Drape was unsure about what to do. He'd been in and out of jail before and knew he didn't want to go back. So, he waited momentarily, then looked into the eyes of the detective wondering, why him?

Out of the blue, Drape mashed down on the gas and

swerved around the ambulance just missing one of the detectives by inches. Going to jail obviously wasn't one of his options. The dope he had on him was enough to get a life sentence and too much money to get confiscated. The only explanation for what was happening to him was that Malik had set him up or they were already following him all day. *Maybe they just decided to make their move*, he thought.

"Damn!" Drape said to himself, noticing that the speedometer had hit 85 mph. He sped through a red light, turning the truck on its left two wheels, avoiding a collision by inches.

"Please stop!" Diona begged as Drape continued to speed.

Drape grasped the steering wheel tightly with his left hand as he leaned over to the passenger side scrambling for the money on the floor. Slightly peering over the dashboard at the road ahead, his speeding intensified as he heard the sirens closely behind. Drape continued to hit top speed with the truck wobbling across the road and every sidewalk. Before long, Diona braced herself knowing they were about to crash.

"Oh my God! Drape please stop!" she shouted.

It was impossible for the Escalade to out run the police cars that were chasing them. Drape knew the first rule to getting away from the police in a chase was to beat the radio. He knew he had to bail out the car before he had the whole police force chasing him. Scouring for the perfect place to bail, he rubbernecked from side to side, asking Diona to pass him the drugs and the money. Unexpectedly, Drape hopped a curb ending up in a field, which sat off the highway, separating the houses from the freeway. He bailed, gripping both bags with the money and the dope, leaving Diona behind.

"Ce'sar Lopez! Stop!" a detective yelled as he tried to give chase.

Drape continued running on some Forrest Gump type

shit never looking back. Unfortunately, the more he ran, Drape eventually had to pitch the bag of dope. Once he was out of sight, he hid under the porch of a house that was near the field. Luckily, the sun had just gone down and he ended up on a street, which appeared to be vacant. The block consisted of a few houses, majority thought to be abandoned, from the lack of activity and lights within the homes.

Exhausted and unable to run any further, his chest burned badly as he gasped for air. He lay under the terrace trying to recuperate, and contemplate his next move. Running another foot seemed impossible. Drape was winded. All of the smoking and drinking night after night with Tim and Romeo had a lot of wear and tear on his buffed frame. Plus the fact that he'd been neglecting his workout didn't help either. Drape had a perfectly carved body with a six-pack, but late night partying put his stamina at an all time low.

Drape all of sudden began to react. He began to stash the $23,000 under the porch as quickly as he could. His heart pulsated so hard he could hear it throbbing loudly. Hiding in one spot too long was something he knew he couldn't do when the police were on his ass.

When five minutes passed and there was no sound of police, he attempted to crawl from under the porch. Slightly peeping from under the house, he noticed Diona's white Escalade slowly approaching. The white man behind the wheel wore a baseball cap and the fact that he was driving his girl's truck made it obvious that they had her in custody. The white man drove down the street at a sluggish pace, hoping for Drape to come out his hiding spot, possibly thinking he was Diona. Drape's main objective now was to separate himself from the money he'd stashed under the porch.

He waited then watched the Escalade turn around hoping to locate Drape. It stopped for a couple of minutes idling half-way up the block. Soon, the truck began to cruise down the street. Drape observed from the dark crawl space as the truck drove further away from him. As soon as it turned the corner, he quickly crawled from under the house. Drape instantly took off running, glancing at the address on the house before he took off, "1425," he kept saying to himself… "1425." Out of breath again, he ran a couple blocks, and jumped a few fences, before pounding on the back door of a house repeatedly.

"Help me! Somebody tried to rob me!" Drape stuttered to the tall dark man in the doorway. He tried to ease his way inside the slightly cracked door.

"Uh uhh, you that muthafucka who all these damn police around here been looking for," the dark man said. He placed his arm against the door frame blocking Drape from coming in any further. He stared Drape up and down examining his ripped shirt and soiled jeans.

Drape reached in his pocket and pulled out the money Malik had given him. He shoved it into the homeowner's hands. "I hope dats enough." When the homeowner nodded his head, Drape slowly eased his way inside the house, thinking, *money is everyone's weakness in the ghetto*.

"Good lookin'," Drape exclaimed with the sound of relief in his voice. Drape began to frisk his hip for his cell phone, but it wasn't there. *Shit I must've dropped it when I was running.* "Is it possible dat I can use yo' phone?" he asked the man.

The happy homeowner pointed to the cordless phone on the table, never taking his eyes off the crumpled money he was straightening out. Drape dialed the first person who came to his mind, the most reliable person that he knew. His hand trembled slightly while he awaited an answer.

"What's da business?" Shorty answered. Her voice was good to hear at a time like this.

"Drape," he said in a low voice. The last thing he needed was for the man to know who he was.

"Why the fuck you breathing so hard?" Shorty asked.

"I need you to do me a favor," Drape said anxiously. "Go to da apartment on Lorain Avenue, look under da sink, and grab dat dope and dat Pyrex. Get rid of 'em. Oh yeah...make sho' you throw dat scale away too. Then come get me," Drape, instructed as he rattled off some other instructions.

"Where you at?" she asked.

"I'll be on the corner of West 60th and Detroit," he replied.

"Got it."

"Shorty hurry, don't take all night. Have yo' trunk popped up before you pull up," he demanded.

"A'ight. You know I'm on it," she ended.

Thirty minutes later Shorty still hadn't arrived. Drape checked his Rolex only to realize it was almost 9:30. He began to think she'd gotten arrested at the apartment. All types of thoughts flooded his head. He stood at the window peeking out into the darkness like a crack head. He even wondered if Malik could've known about his cook-up apartment. Then a smile appeared on his face as he watched Shorty's Lexus RX 300 pull slowly in the front. *Like clockwork, she's always on point*, he thought. Before leaving, Drape turned to the tall dark man, and with a mean scowl and said, "You didn't fuckin' see me!"

Rushing out the front door and climbing into her trunk, Drape eyed the homeowner as he left. Quickly, Shorty raced to the highway and headed to the eastside of Cleveland in silence; simply re-applying her make-up to look good for Drape. Twenty minutes later, she pulled into the Garden Valley projects and parked. Shorty hopped her sexy red-bone ass out the car with her butt cheeks peeking from her jean, booty shorts. After checking the area closely, she popped the trunk, and watched Drape climb out. He'd messed up the paperwork showcasing the houses that she'd planned on showing her clients later, but it wasn't a good time to fuss.

"What the fuck happened?" she asked as she observed

his clothes.

"They got her," Drape said in a low tone.

"Got who?" Shorty inquired, pulling her long hair off her neck.

"Diona, I can't let dem charge her wit' shit. Dat shit would fuck her whole life up. Damn! I gotta turn myself in."

"Damn." Shorty hit him with the one word response, then licked her glossy lips. Her only concern was Drape.

While Drape paced back and forth nervously, Shorty stood in place trying to figure out what actually happened. She didn't give a fuck about Diona, but had never seen Drape so paranoid and shaken up before. The way he was acting, she figured it had to be serious. He usually kept his cool in the worse situations.

"And I had to stash twenty three grand underneath somebody's fuckin' porch. Remember this address…1425," he rambled.

Shorty nodded her head. "Got it."

Unexpectedly, Drape grabbed her cell phone from out of the car and began dialing.

"Hello," the man answered groggily.

"Byron dis Drape, I need yo' help. I got Diona in some trouble!"

"What kind of trouble? Where's my fucking daughter?" Diona's father asked. "By the way who told you to call me by my first name? I never approved that."

Drape knew now wasn't the time to go toe to toe with someone he needed help from. "Sorry Mr. Young. Da police got her."

"What police?"

"I don't know! I think it is da Second District."

Malik lived in the vicinity, so Drape figured it had to be the Second District police station. If anybody could help her, it would have to be her father. He was one of the biggest and prestigious criminal attorneys in the city. Drape knew by asking for this favor, he would fry in exchange for Diona. Her father never accepted the fact that Diona loved Drape, however he knew that he couldn't control Diona's feelings either.

"Where the hell are you?" Mr. Young asked.

"I'm on East 79th Street, in da Garden Valley Projects."

"Stay there. Don't go any fucking where." His voice raged. "I'm on my way!"

SNITCH

Mr. Young must've sped through every red light on his way because by the time Drape explained to Shorty what happened, Diona's father was turning into the parking lot.

"Good lookin' out baby girl," Drape said thanking Shorty, and then giving her a hug.

Once in the car, Drape could see that Mr. Young still had on his pajamas as he put on his seatbelt as instructed. Drape's mind drifted as they drove and Mr. Young gave him the third degree. All he could think about is what they had on him and how much it would cost to beat the case. Asking Mr. Young for help on this one was out of the question. He had burned his bridges with him completely.

Apparently on the way to the Garden Valley Projects, Mr. Young had called and gotten in touch with the detectives who had Diona in custody. He arranged for Drape to turn himself in. Any charges they had on Diona would be dropped in exchange for Drape. Drape had dodged many bullets in life, but that was about to change. When they arrived at the police station several minutes later, it looked like a Klu Klux Klan rally because all the white detectives appeared racist, especially when they applauded as Drape began to make his way toward them.

"What da fuck I done got myself into?" Drape thought to

himself. He couldn't do anything but expect the worse and hope for the best. He prayed they hadn't found the dope he'd thrown. It was time to see what charges they had on him. Diona stood next to one of the detectives in handcuffs with eyes that were both puffy and blood shot red. Seeing her in this situation made him feel like a piece of shit. Everything Diona said earlier had just blown up in his face at that very moment. The woman he loved was caught up in his bullshit, yet she despised his hustling to the fullest. He couldn't believe he had put her in such a bad predicament. Hustling with her was something he knew he shouldn't have been doing. He was being selfish by trying to kill two birds with one stone.

A detective grabbed Drape tightly by his arm and began to walk him toward the front entrance of the station. He lowered his head in shame. "What kind of coward bails and leaves his girlfriend?" The detective signified loud enough for Diona to hear him as they walked past her.

"I love you Diona!" Drape shouted.

"Yeah, I love me too!" Diona mumbled loud enough for Drape to hear."You'll see," she added in disgust. Diona just looked at Drape with a pair of cold eyes, which pierced his heart. For the first time, Drape saw a side to Diona that he'd never seen before. *It was clear; she was tired of his bullshit.*

CHAPTER 5

Drape sat in the county jail for three days waiting to be charged so he could appear in bond court, hoping to post bond. While he sat in the jail, he called his boy that he confided in most, Tim… and told him to call Shorty. He needed her to disconnect the cell phone he'd lost while running since it was in her name. He also needed her to be at the courthouse with his lawyer so she could sign his bond. He'd always stashed bond money over her house in case of situations like this. When Drape walked into the courtroom, he noticed Shorty and his attorney sitting in the back row.

"Ce'sar Lopez!" the judge shouted holding a docket in his hand.

It was Drape's turn to go to the podium. He rose up off the long bench of convicts and approached the podium with his lawyer by his side. They were ready to hear what the prosecutor had to say, who sat across from them. When the prosecutor stood up from the table and began fumbling through the papers in front of him, a lump formed in Drape's throat.

"The State of Ohio versus Ce'sar Lopez your honor. The state is charging Mr. Lopez with drug trafficking five hundred grams of cocaine base crack, a felony in the first degree, felonious assault with a deadly weapon in the first degree, and obstruction of official business, your honor," the prosecutor stated.

After hearing his charges, he knew the police didn't find the dope he'd thrown.

"Mr. Lopez, are you aware you have the right to wave your preliminary hearing? Would you like to wave, yes or no?" the judge asked.

"Yes your honor," Drape replied, after his lawyer gave him a nudge and a nod. Drape remembered if he didn't wave his preliminary hearing, the judge would've ordered him to be detained until he had it.

"How does your client plead to these charges, Mr. Goldstein?"

"My client enters a plea of not guilty your honor."

"Bail set at a hundred thousand, no cash surety," the judge stated as he slammed his gavel.

Drape's lawyer leaned in close and said, "Call me when you get home."

During bond court, Drape recognized Malik's girlfriend Tina and her cousin sitting on the bench of female offenders, waiting to hear what they were going to be charged with. He avoided eye contact with them because it was obvious that he was being charged with the half of key he'd fronted Malik. With them facing charges, there was no telling what they were capable of saying. The only thing he couldn't figure out was where Malik was and why he wasn't in court and they were.

As soon as his lawyer walked off, a bailiff escorted him back to the bullpen. The smell of the urine reeked as Drape flopped restlessly on the hard plastic mattress. The rattling of the bars when the guard pulled them shut ignited his phobia of being claustrophobic. He laid there with his hands behind his head as he shut his eyes, exhausted from the lack of sleep over the past three days. Drape thought of Diona as he dozed off.

Forty-five minutes into his light nap, a voice sounded. "Lopez!" the guard yelled as he opened the cell bars.

Drape got up and hastily made his way out of the cell. He knew that Shorty must've gotten the ten thousand he needed and given it to a bail bondsman.

SNITCH

"Drape pay our bonds!" Malik's girlfriend Tina yelled as she caught a glimpse of him walking by the women's cell.

He continued to walk pass as if he never heard her and without looking back. When he got outside, Shorty was waiting in her car with a fresh rolled blunt and his new cell phone, a small black, Motorola flip phone. It was three things a man wanted as soon as he got out of jail: a blunt, some real food, and some pussy. Being the street bitch she was, she already knew this.

"Damn, I need some weed," Drape said as he got in Shorty's car.

"Here," she said handing him a blunt, and pulling off with one thing on her mind.

The ride was mostly silent between Shorty and Drape since he'd spent the entire time trying to contact his boys. He called Tim first. When he didn't answer, he tried Tiger.

"What up nigga?" Drape asked.

"Nigga you a'ight? What da fuck happened?" Tiger asked with concern.

"For now, I'm wit' Shorty on my way to her spot. They just released me. You ain't gon' believe dis shit," Drape replied.

"Nigga what they talkin' bout? How long you gon' be ova' there? We need to link up."

"Dis shit crazy, I'll tell you later. Where everybody at?"

"They gettin' money...handlin' business!"

"A'ight. I'll call you when I come out."

"A'ight my nigga!" Tiger said, hanging up.

Once they pulled into Shorty's driveway, they exited the car, and walked toward the entrance of her apartment. Drape followed Shorty into the house admiring her shapely ass as she switched hard from side to side. Nothing had changed; her walk was still nasty. Drape was overwhelmed with being horny and hungry. As soon as they got inside Shorty stripped down to her Victoria's Secret panties and matching bra, and Drape instantly went at her.

"Hold up," she objected, and then pushed him off of her. "Why?"

"Nigga, yo' ass ain't washed up in three days. You not about to stick that dirty dick up in me! You better go take yo' ass and get in the shower first," Shorty said pointing to the bathroom. She chuckled to herself as Drape walked toward the bathroom.

Like a certified chef, Shorty walked up to the refrigerator, grabbed two lobster tails and two potatoes. She then cut the lobster out the tails, seasoned them extra good, adding butter and a little garlic, Drape's favorite. When she finished she wrapped them in aluminum foil and slipped them both into the broiler with a smile before heading into the bathroom.

Drape was already in the tub soaking when Shorty walked in. She began to take her bra and panties off seductively as if she were performing a striptease act. Drape's dick rose out of the suds as soon as Shorty stepped into the tub and mounted herself on top of him. She grabbed his hard dick and began to rub it against her clit until her juices flowed.

"I'm glad you're out," she told him seductively.

"Show me," he shot back.

Drape was ready and didn't quite know what Shorty was up to. She flickered her tongue for several seconds before hopping off Drape and dropping to her knees. Sexily, she bent over, taking every inch of Drape's dick into her mouth. She drenched his pipe with her saliva causing him to yell out with pleasure.

"Oh shit!" he shouted.

His butt cheeks rose from the base of the tub, but Shorty never stopped. Every time she deep throated his shaft with her mouth, she also stroked his shaft with her left hand, something Drape loved. Her mouth moved rhythmically up and down while Drape's eyes rolled in his head, caressing her long locks of hair. She deep throated his love stick repeatedly causing him to lose his mind.

"Ahhhh shit!" he squirmed. "Damnnnnnn," he said through clenched teeth.

Suddenly, Shorty stopped. She mounted Drape as he cupped her breast covered in suds. She then slid down on his magic stick and began to buck like a wild horse. She moaned and made noises like a porn star. "Fuck me Drape!" she called out. Drape grunted and fucked harder as Shorty egged him on. "Harder! Harder!" she shouted.

Drape obliged and held her down by her waist as they both busted massive nuts. Moments later, Shorty got up like the sex was nothing and pranced into her bedroom. She allowed her wet body to air dry as she laid across her bed seductively. Drape followed with a towel wrapped around his waist wondering why she wasn't somebody's number one by the way she gave head. Before she could even get up to fix him a plate, Drape was already in the kitchen eating his lobster tail out of the broiler. He came back into the bedroom, sat on the corner of her bed, and began to put his clothes back on.

Shorty finally got up, grabbed a bag out of the closet and tossed it to him. He opened the bag and flashed a grin before pulling out the new outfit, socks and boxers. "Those are yours too," she said pointing to a fresh pair of Air Force One's in a shoebox on her dresser. "I'm throwing this shit away," Shorty informed as she picked up his ripped shirt and soiled jeans with just two fingers, throwing them into a plastic bag. She had this escapade planned the day Tim called her and said that Drape had gotten locked up. She knew he would need her just as he always did.

After Drape was dressed, she drove him to Angel's house, so he could take him home. Shorty didn't want to start no shit between him and Diona out of love for Drape. When they pulled up in front of Angel's, Shorty had a saddened expression on her face.

"This shit is getting old Drape," she said out of the blue. "Five years is too long."

"I thought we had an understandin.'" He hit Shorty with a fatherly look.

"We do. I'm just bored wit' this shit."

"C'mon Shorty. Not now, okay? We straight?" he asked, hoping to dismiss her whining.

"Yeah. We straight , Drape. Now, get the fuck out."

The Shorty situation had never been a problem in the past. Drape always told Diona he and Shorty were best friends, more like brother and sister since childhood. Diona accepted that for his sake, but a woman's intuition was always right. She always felt deep inside they were fucking, but couldn't prove it. Shorty on the other hand seemed to be catching deeper feelings.

Angel was glad to see his brother come through the door. It wasn't often that they had a chance to hang out; just the two of them. So even if it was covering for his brother that was fine with him. Angel drove his brother home asking tons of questions along the way about the dope game and how Drape got caught. When they walked through the door, Diona was shocked. He hadn't called her in the three days he'd spent in county jail.

"Hey baby!" he shouted excitedly while embracing her.

"Don't hey baby me. What the fuck were you thinking? You got me over here waiting for your punk ass to see what's going on and you prance through the door three days later. I called Tim, and Tiger trying to figure out what the hell was going on.

"I know baby," was all Drape could say.

"I guess you called your girl in your time of need while I sat here looking stupid."

"C'mon baby, I thought you were mad at me especially after what you said at da station."

"You're full of shit, Drape." Then she paused, checking

out his clothes. "Wow, a fresh new outfit! You know what…please don't ever think you got one up on me. This shit is becoming too much for me, I don't need the stress." Diona walked away remembering that she hadn't spoken to Angel. "What's up Angel?"

"Hey Diona," he chimed, then took a seat in front of the flat screen. Angel really was a big time television fan, but Diona figured he didn't want any parts of their arguing.

"What do you think my parents will have to say about this? Don't you think I'm tired of them telling me how much of a no good nigga you are! Where's my damn car? I could've lost my life, but your petty ass money is worth more. You know what...fuck you and that bitch."

When Diona began to cry Drape took two steps in her direction, but she stepped backward.

"I'm so sorry Diona, I love you so much. I just made a fucked up decision. I need you and our baby in my life. I know I messed up, but don't leave me, please," Drape pleaded.

"Whateva Drape. Shut your trifling ass up because I don't wanna hear it."

Drape felt fucked up about the situation. To know she was hurt, made him hurt. Everything was so surreal and risking Diona and his baby for the streets wasn't worth any amount of money or bitch. Being that he had just fucked Shorty didn't make him feel any better. He knew Diona took a lot of shit, much he thought she didn't know about. He wondered how she knew Shorty picked him up. That day, his whole mentality changed. He wanted better for himself, especially his child.

Drape wondered who had been talking to Diona and running his or her mouth about his business. Drape knew it was some shit in the game, but he would certainly find out *who* and *why*.

SNITCH

CHAPTER 6

Two days later, Drape's Motorola vibrated on the night-stand loudly at 7:30 a.m.

"What's da business?" Drape asked groggily.

"Drape, I have some bad news," Mr. Goldstein uttered.

He instantly hopped out of bed, lowered the volume on his phone and then walked into the bathroom, caressing his dick through his boxers. He didn't want Diona to hear what was about to be said. Little did he know, she'd opened one eye as he walked away from the bed.

"What's da bad news?" Drape asked as butterflies filled his stomach.

"The Feds picked up your case."

"Man don't tell me dat. I just got out. How dat happen so fast?"

"They're here at my office right now."

"What! Who you workin' for, 'dem or me? I can't believe dis shit is happenin'!"

Mr. Goldstein assured him that he wouldn't be arrested if he came to his office, but if he didn't come, a federal arrest warrant would be issued. Drape took a deep breath as he pondered the thought of what could happen when he got there.

"Fuck it, I'm on my way," he said hanging up.

He came out of the bathroom and got dressed quietly as Diona laid in the bed with her eyes closed pretending to be sleep. Once he was dressed, he leaned over and kissed her on the cheek and left. She was barely speaking to him and he was trying his hardest not to upset her anymore.

Drape drove his low-key Honda Accord to his lawyer's office playing out different scenarios in his head the entire ride. Once he arrived, he drove a block away from Mr. Goldstein's and parked. He thought it was best to walk the rest of the way just in case they tried to arrest him; knowing he would make a run for it. As soon as he walked into Mr. Goldstein's plush office, his secretary was in the foyer area sitting at her desk. She escorted Drape to the conference room where Mr. Goldstein was expecting him.

"How are you Ce'sar?" he greeted. "This is Detective Burns from the Cleveland Police Department, Narcotics division...Second District. I think you two have met before," Mr. Goldstein said.

Drape's thick eyebrows crinkled. Detective Burns looked like the young detective who'd jumped out of the ambulance. Drape looked at the ugly keloid scar on Detective Burns' cheek and thought how demented it made his face look. Burns was a frail looking guy appearing to be in his early twenties. He wondered what could've happened to someone so young to make their appearance be so abnormal. Drape chuckled inside at the thought of Burns, a rookie, who was way too inexperienced to be dealing with him.

"And I'm Agent Lewis from the F.B.I," another man said, introducing himself. Agent Lewis looked like a hill-billy with blonde hair and blue eyes. "I'm gonna be working with Detective Burns on this case. Mr. Lopez, can I call you Drape?" Lewis asked with a toothpick lodged in his teeth.

"Yeah, it's cool." Drape anxiously waited to hear what the agent had to say.

"By the way, why do they call you Drape?"

Drape smiled. "Because I stay draped in some fly shit."

"That's funny," Lewis chuckled, then looked at Burns

SNITCH

hoping to get a laugh out of him. He got nothing but a straight face.

"I'm going to get straight to the point. Help us help you. We got wire taps and surveillance of you at Malik Howard's house selling him 500 grams of cocaine base crack," he said.

Agent Lewis exposed Malik to Drape at ease because he knew there was nothing he could do about it. There was no way he could hurt or intimidate him because he was currently in protective custody. They'd taken extra precautions to keep him safe. Without Malik, the dope and the wiretaps weren't enough to convict Drape. Agent Lewis informed him that he and the Scrilla Boys had been under investigation for the past three months, and they had a secret informant making a controlled buy from his younger brother, Angel.

"Fuck," Drape said under his breath. He'd told Angel to leave that shit alone. "Who da fuck was servin' him?" Drape asked himself. He then focused back on his situation. Even though he was sure Tina and her cousin, Dee Dee didn't see the transaction; he knew they would take the stand against him if he went to trial. The Feds were good in coercing witnesses.

Drape crossed his arms on the table and let out a sigh as he laid his head down on his muscular arms. He thought silently to himself for a second then raised his head. "What da fuck do y'all want me to do?" he asked as if he'd lost the war.

"We want the Scrilla Boys off the streets and we want you to make control buys from them on wire. I don't care who the drugs get sold to as long as it's on wire," Agent Lewis said firmly, and then took a sip of water from the cup in front of him.

Drape's heart sank. He couldn't believe they wanted him to rat on his own crew; his boys that he'd known since childhood. The crew who always had his back. He sighed then let out a sign of disgust.

"Fuck naw! I'on think I'ma be able to do dat.' He gazed off to the side and fell into a frenzied looking daze.

VegasClarke

Lewis played around with his toothpick again. "Call me after you've thought for a couple of days. Your lawyer will inform you on how much time you're facing." Agent Lewis handed Drape his card, and then headed for the door with Detective Burns in tow. "You know it's you or them," he added.

Instead of responding, Drape turned away.

Mr. Goldstein escorted them to the door as Drape sat defeated, in deep thought. He came back into his office within seconds, and pulled a chair next to him. "Drape, these charges carry a mandatory minimum of twenty years and a maximum of life in prison. The Feds have a ninety-eight percent conviction rate and with your record, we don't stand a chance in trial. A plea would still get you at least twenty years or more. It's your choice. The balls in your court," Mr. Goldstein said in a matter of fact tone.

Drape half-listened as he daydreamed. Finally, he turned his head to his attorney and said, "I'll call and let you know what I'm gonna do."

Mr. Goldstein sighed "Fine with me."

Drape got up and left. For nearly thirty minutes, he sat in his car and contemplated if he should do what the Feds wanted. Snitching was going against the grain; he knew it could cost him his life or even worse, his families'. He was the one who enforced the Scrilla Boys code that if somebody snitched, they were to be killed. He broke out into a frustrated rage and began to beat his fist against the steering wheel repeatedly.

Romeo, Tim, and Tiger were his brothers, he told himself. Family was everything. Then his thoughts switched to Diona. She was his heart. Drape started the engine as he had visions of his child being born and him not being there. He beat against the wheel again, then drove off. The only thing that was going through his mind was Diona and his unborn child as he sped off.

SNITCH

SNITCH

Nine days passed since Drape had gotten out of jail and seven since he'd spoken to the Feds at his lawyer's office. Diona was at a doctor's appointment so he moped around the house smoking blunt after blunt while guzzling down Hennessey straight out of a bottle. He'd been thinking about the Fed's ultimatum all week, and everything seemed to be a problem. He knew his connect would be calling with some bricks soon. And even though he could dump most of his work off to the Scrilla Boys, the fact that they were under investigation was a major dilemma. Drape didn't want to take a risk serving them and catching another case. Something had to be done and he had to do it fast. He'd only made $15,000 off of the two bricks he bought off of Peanut. That was a $27,000 loss, really a $29,000 loss if he counted the extra two grand Peanut slicked him out of. He was used to making major money and having the finer things in life. He'd decided nothing was going to stop him. He devised a plan, picked up his cell phone, and began dialing.

"What's poppin'?" Tim answered.

Tim was the one out the crew who couldn't hold water. Anything that was told to him would surely be repeated to someone else. He was a Scrilla Boy because he was a flat foot hustler and he didn't have a problem busting his gun.

"Dawg somebody hit my spot. Me and Diona came home last night and the fuckin' door was wide open," Drape replied.

"Who da fuck you think did it?"

"Shit if I know, a nigga should be strappin' up to go kill somethin'. After all 'dem stick ups I done, I can't accept it when da shit happens to me."

"What they get?"

"A nice chunk of change. You know a nigga don't like talkin' over these phones. I'll just see you tonight at da Mirage. I need da club right about now."

"Aight, but you watch yo'self."

By the time Drape hung up, called his lawyer and called Shorty, time had flown. He knew that if he could trust anybody knowing he was going to cooperate with the Feds, it was Shorty. Drape let her know every aspect of his plan and what he needed her to do to help him pull off their hoodwink. He told her word for word what the Feds had said. A part of the plan was to get the bricks from his connect and give them to her. Shorty would then contact Tim, letting him know she knew somebody who had the bricks for the low. Once Tim would contact Drape and the crew, they would put their money together and purchase some work from her. In order for it to go down like that, he and Shorty had to portray to be on bad terms. The Scrilla Boys knew how close they were, and if she had somebody with some work, she would hit Drape off and he would be able to hit them off. Drape was going to act as if his connect didn't break him off with any work.

Shorty pulling down on the Scrilla Boys wouldn't be out the ordinary. She was known for fuckin' with big time dope dealers. From time to time, she would catch her a nigga with that work for cheap at an All-Star weekend or an awards show. That was how they used to get most of their victims. Drape was about to try to kill two birds with one stone and make money doing it.

Shorty listened intently but thought the shit was foul. However, her love for Drape outweighed it all. Especially when he told her that he had some money for her. They kicked it a little while longer listening to Drape explain how he had to cut the emotional ties with his boys. "It's either them, or me," he told Shorty.

"Ummm huh." Tim was the only one of his friends that she liked anyway.

"So we straight," he concluded. "Meet me at the *Mirage on the Water.*"

Shorty didn't mind. It was one of the most popular night-clubs in Cleveland. If anybody was somebody, they were there on Sunday nights with their best on. Shorty knew she had an opportunity to catch her a new baller and Drape knew it was the best place for him and Shorty to make their initial move.

SNITCH

Drape pulled up to the club in his cocaine white 500SL Mercedes Benz on chrome twenty-one inch rims. He hopped out in the valet zone, leaving the car running and music blasting.

"Here, make sure my shit stay parked out front," he demanded, sliding the valet a crisp fifty.

He arrogantly strolled to the front of the long line of people who were waiting to go into the club dressed in a Hugo Boss button down shirt, True Religion jeans, and a pair of Prada tennis shoes. Drape whispered a few words in the bouncer's ear before walking through the ropes and going inside the club.

Bone Crushers', *"Never Scared"* thumped loudly through the speakers as he made his way through the over-crowded dance floor. It didn't take long before he spotted Shorty and her best friend Porsha at the bar glued to the Scrilla Boys and the many bottles of champagne that lined the bar's counter. Shorty stood out in her off the shoulder Chanel top showing every bit of her cleavage, and skintight Seven Jeans, which hugged her perfectly shaped plump ass. Not to mention, the jeans complimented her long legs.

Porsha, who was also Tim's baby mama stood beside Shorty like a true sidekick showcasing the cursive tattoo that read, *Tim*, on the side of her neck. She had a long blond wig down her back and wore a black bustier and ripped Chloe Jeans. Porsha was also a red bone like Shorty, and behaved just as wild as she did.

VegasClarke

"Wassup my nigga!" Romeo yelled over the loud music as Drape approached.

Drape noticed that Romeo had added another tattoo to the side of his neck, this one even flashier than before; two dollar signs with orange and red flames. He wanted to say something, but it wasn't the time. All of the Scrilla Boys huddled around him with deep concern and empathy. It was obvious Tim had informed them of the bad news.

"What happened? You a'ight?" Romeo asked.

"C'mon, y'all already know what happened," he winced. Then he looked at Tim and said, "Everything cool, a nigga gone bounce back."

They knew he'd taken a loss, but they also knew that didn't mean he was broke. It was known all over town that Drape had big money.

"Let me get five bottles of Cristal!" Drape yelled to the bartender.

"Uh hell no!" Shorty protested loudly. "No he didn't. He ought to be giving me my fucking money. I'm about to flip the fuck out," Shorty said to Porsha and loud enough for the fellas to hear. She crossed her arms and shifted her weight from one leg to another. She stared angrily at him for ordering the five bottles of Cristal.

Drape turned around after paying the bartender and caught eye contact with her. Shorty stepped in close to him, "Damn nigga if you doing it like that, pay a bitch her money with yo' fronting balla ass!" All eyes were on them as they argued loudly in each other's face.

"Bitch fuck you! I ain't payin' you shit now, just fo dat," he fired back.

"Oh, nigga you gone pay me mine!"

"Only way you gone get yo money from me is how Tyson got his title, hoe!" Drape said feeling pimpish.

He and Shorty were close enough to kiss as they put on

a scene. For a minute, Drape thought about how strong Shorty was talking to him. She was serious like it wasn't planned. She could have won an Oscar for her performance.

"Chill out," Tiger said stepping in between them, "Lemme' holla at you," he said to Drape as he pulled him out of her face. Shorty and Drape continued to argue as Tiger managed to pull him to the side. "Dawg, I know you gotta a lot of shit on yo' mind, but you trippin'," Tiger continued. "You and me go way back. You my dawg, but this shit ain't important right now."

"You know what, you right. Shit is all fucked up for me right now. I ain't got no money fo' dis club shit right now and no time to be arguin' wit' dis bitch." Drape stopped to give a strong sigh of frustration. "I just can't believe she tried to front a nigga in da club about a petty ass ten g's. She know I'ma pay her dat shit. I ain't givin' her shit now, fuck her! Matter of fact, I'ma go over to da other side of the bar and chill wit' some other bitches," Drape said leaving Tiger standing in the corner alone.

By 2 a.m., Shorty was standing by her car talking Tim and Romeo's ears off about how she'd loaned Drape ten g's to bond him out of jail. She went on and on saying that she and Drape never needed to speak from now on. While passing her, Drape shot a mean mug at Shorty on his way to valet. She returned his mean mug along with a middle finger.

"Fuck you," she mouthed.

Drape chuckled to himself as he walked to his car thinking how good him and Shorty's plan had gone. They were truly Bonnie and Clyde. It was time for his next move, but how well it would go, depended on Shorty's gritty, conniving ass.

SNITCH

CHAPTER 7

The next day, Tim pulled up to Shorty's hair salon for his once a week hair braiding appointment in his Lexus GS 400. Along with the car, the chrome spinning rims labeled him a certified baller. Her salon windows were graced with pink neon lights and the salon's name, *"Hair Doo's"* was lit up in purple neon lighting. *"Hair Doo's"* was your average ghetto salon in the hood. While getting your hair done, you could hear everything from who was fucking whose man to who got the latest baller, pussy whipped.

Tim took a drag off his blunt then sat it in the ashtray. He then got out of his car taking a step back to look into his spotless window before straightening out his fresh, new Polo attire. The brother was Polo crazy always rocking the newest line. *A nigga gotta be on point walking into a hair salon full of hoes*, he thought to himself. He knew they would surely check him out from head to toe. *Looking good as usual*, he thought to himself as he hit his chirp on his car alarm and walked inside.

Shorty was the only one in the shop. She swept around her booth as Tim came through the door with a smile. "Damn, you look like shit."

"Fuck you nigga," Shorty shot back.

Even though she still managed to apply her favorite fuchsia lip gloss and bronzer, the way she was dressed displayed how she felt when she woke up from a long night of drinking and clubbing. The fly ass hair style she had the night before was now in a wrap with a multi-colored scarf wrapped around it and the massive Cleveland Cavilers t-shirt she wore looked like it belonged to her uncle. Even though she didn't look like her normal self, you could still see her shapely figure in the loose jogging paints she had on.

"Smoke something wit' a bitch," she suggested after getting a whiff of the weed smell that reeked from his clothes.

"I gotta blunt in da ash tray. Go get it and we can blow," Tim replied as he dangled his car keys from his hand.

"Damn boy, yo' ass is so lazy," Shorty said sucking on her teeth as she snatched the keys out of his hand. She shoved the broom into his chest.

It was two things Shorty adored, clothes and weed. Within a dash, she came back into the shop and locked the door behind her.

"Where da hoes at?" Tim asked, upset that there was no one in the shop to floss in front of.

"Sit yo' half-white ass down."

Shorty shut the blinds, then changed the opened sign to closed. In actuality, Tim was her last customer for the day due to the pounding headache she couldn't get rid off from the night before. She'd been up doing hair since 8'o clock that morning, so some rest was desperately needed.

"Damn, this some fire," she said after letting out a harsh cough, then passed the blunt.

"Yeah dis dat dro', not dat bullshit you be smokin'," Tim bragged.

Shorty tapped the back of her booth chair letting him know to take a seat. After taking off the rubber band that held his shoulder length hair in place she paused. "Did you wash this shit? I hope so."

"Damn is dat how you treat yo' clients? Yeah, I washed it."

"Good because I didn't feel like it," Shorty said as she took one of her rat tailed combs and parted a section of his hair. "Tim, be straight up wit' me," Shorty pleaded with her boobs touching the top of his head, "Is Drape ever gonna leave Diona?"

"C'mon now, Shorty. You from the streets, you know the game. Don't tell me you fallin?" He licked his full set of darkened lips. "I thought y'all was on the outs?"

"We are. I'm done wit' him. I'm just curious."

"Whatever Shorty. Y'all gon be cool in a couple of days. Watch."

"I doubt that shit." Shorty pressed her lips together sassily.

"Especially when you need some dick."

She pushed Tim's head playfully. "No serious," she said giving off a solemn look, "A bitch gotta settle down one day. It definitely won't be with Drape's bitch ass, but I mean I might wanna have kids."

Tim looked down at her long shapely legs that he could envision even through her sweats. "And mess up that banging ass body? Naw, Shorty, save that for the housewives. You know Drape can't turn no hoe into a housewife." He laughed as Shorty pushed his head again.

Thirty minutes into another good conversation and feeling a buzz, Shorty decided it was the perfect time to put her and Drape's plan into action.

"Tim, I know Drape ain't been having any work lately and you know damn well I don't fuck wit' muthafuckas, but one of my niggas got bricks for cheap. The only reason I'm pulling down on you is because you a good nigga," she said stroking his ego and braiding tightly all at the same time.

"Why you ain't get at Drape?" Tim gave off a puzzled expression.

"Real funny muthafucka! You know that nigga still

owe me ten g's for bonding his scandalous ass out. Plus, he more focused on Diona than me. Now he can keep his petty money after he showed his ass last night."

"So, what's cheap?" he asked.

"Twenty g's a brick."

Tim raised his eyebrows. "Damn dat's high."

"Nigga please! Drape was charging yo' ass more than that. So don't even try that bullshit. Good game, wrong bitch." All Tim could do was laugh. "Nigga just call me when you're ready."

"Damn yo' ass think you hip to everything. I'ma call you in a couple of days."

Tim sat fretfully as she finished his braids. As soon as he got into his car, he called Drape to inform him of what Shorty had just informed him. He then told Drape to meet him at *Lancers Steakhouse Bar* because it was urgent.

CHAPTER 8

Tim sped to *Lancers* a half restaurant half bar where the Scrilla Boys hung out often. He was anxious to see what Drape's reaction would be to what Shorty had just told him. He was hoping Drape gave him the green light to rob her. It had been two years since the Scrilla Boys put their stick up game down, and he was hungry for a new victim. Fortunately, Drape already knew what the urgency was. As Drape rushed through *Lancers'* front door, he spotted Tim sitting at the bar. The lights in the ceiling reflected a glare off Tim's fresh greasy braids. He recognized Drape approaching from behind as he peered through the mirror behind the bar.

He spun around on the bar stool, "Whassup dawg?" he said excitedly. He was feeling the drink he had before Drape arrived.

"What's so damn important?" Drape said playing stupid.

"I went up to Shorty's shop to get my hair braided like I do every week, right."

"Yeah I can tell," Drape joked as he stared at his shiny braids.

"Why you say dat?" Tim remarked with a huge smile on his face. His head was toward Drape, but his eyes cut toward the mirror conceitedly.

"Damn, white boy! What happened when you went to her shop? What…you got dat Eddie Murphy Soul Glo shit up in there?"

"Fuck you nigga," Tim said snapping out of his trance. "Anyway, she pulled down on me talkin' about some nigga she fuck wit got 'dem bricks fo' twenty a key. I asked her why she ain't get at you. She said she ain't fuckin wit' you about you know what."

"Oh, she did huh, I got somethin' fo' dat bitch. Meet me at Nita's crib around five o'clock. Call everybody and tell 'em to be there."

"What you got in mind?" Tim asked eager to pull a stick up.

"Shit, fo' right now, since my people ain't been comin' through wit' dat work, we need da dope. So, we just gone cop some work from Shorty and when my connect hit me, we gone stick her ass up, fuck it."

"Whew!" Tim said as he rubbed his hands together. "Another stick up. Yes! Been a long time coming."

"Make sure you be there and call everybody and let them know to be there," Drape uttered then walked off.

"Fo' sho'." Tim grinned inward before he took one last gulp of his drink.

Drape sat in his car outside of *Lancer's* for a hot second then went in his pocket and pulled out Agent Lewis' card. He dialed him up as he pulled away from the curb.

"Hello, Agent Lewis speaking."

"Yeah, dis Drape."

"I thought you would never call," he said knowing he was anticipating the call. He held his finger up to his lips letting the other agents in the background know to quiet down. "What you got for me?"

"We havin' a meetin' tonight on how much dope we gone buy from da connect."

"I need to know all the specifics," Agent Lewis replied.

Agent Lewis arranged for Drape to meet him at a Wal-mart on West Boulevard in thirty minutes. He was eager to get more information and get the ball rolling on his investigation. Drape sat around contemplating what he was about to do and what would happen if the Scrilla Boys found what he was up to. As thoughts of him snitching flooded his mind, all he could do was chant those famous words over and over. *It's either them or me.*

SNITCH!!

He turned into the Wal-mart parking lot where Agent Lewis was already waiting for him. It wasn't long before he observed Lewis' country looking appearance sitting in a dark blue Taurus. Drape pulled on the side of him hesitantly and scoped the scene to make sure no familiar faces were around. He then pulled his Cleveland Indians pro model baseball cap over his eyes, got out of his car, and quickly hopped into Agent Lewis' passenger seat. Drape thought it was crazy how Lewis had a toothpick lodged between his teeth once again.

"You're making the right decision," Lewis said, persuading him to follow through with his cooperation.

"Look, save da fuckin' pep talk," Drape said as Agent Lewis handed him a small black box that resembled a pager. "What's dis?"

"It's a recording device."

"Dis bullshit ain't gone work," Drape grumbled in doubt. *I can't do this shit*, he thought.

"We got you didn't we?" Lewis shot back with a smirk, then pulled a piece of his stringy hair out of his face. "We need evidence, and this is the best way to get it."

Drape thought when informants wore wires they were small speakers attached and taped to the chest of the snitch like in the movies. Agent Lewis gave him instructions on what he needed and how he was to wear the wire to the meeting tonight. After that they'd have a strong start on building on a conspiracy case against Tim, Tiger, and Romeo.

As Drape gave directions to where they were having the meeting and what time, Detective Burns pulled up in a black Taurus.

"Take that with you and I'll get it back after the meeting. Meet me back here," Agent Lewis said as Drape got out of the car and Detective Burns hopped in.

Drape frowned at the look Burns gave him. He felt as if his stare was too personal.*Dat nigga just jealous cuz I got money*, he told himself as he eyed him back with the same set of cold eyes.

"It's always da black cops who got a chip on they fuckin' shoulder," Drape told them with a smirk, trying to be sarcastic.

"Just make this work," Lewis ordered.

When Drape got back in his car, the caller I.D on his cell phone displayed three missed calls. Before he could check the calls, his cell phone rang. "Wifey" blinked on the screen as it rang representing Diona's name tag.

"Whassup baby?" he answered.

"Why didn't you answer your phone? Is everything alright? What time will you be here?" she asked out of concern.

"I'm okay. My phone was in my car while I stepped out for a minute. Whassup?"

She switched her tone to sound sad, "Nothing, about to run some errands."

"I should be there no later than eight o'clock or nine. Why, you need somethin'? Is the baby a'ight?"

"I'm okay. The baby's fine too. Been kicking all day."

Hearing Diona talk about baby kicking made Drape very aggravated. He knew that he had a good woman and wanted to be there for her and the baby.

"I promise all dis will be over real soon."

"I'll see you when you get here, I love you," she uttered in a cheerless tone ignoring his last comment. She knew Drape was wrong, but her heart and mind was still pure and she could never be vindictive. Her love was truly genuine.

"I love you, too," he stated then hung up.

Diona's call was the nail in the coffin. He wasn't about to take any chances on loosing her because of a prison term. As hard as it was going to be, now he knew he had to take his boys down.

SNITCH

At exactly five o'clock Drape pulled up to Nita's crib. The row of luxury cars lined up out front of Nita's house looked just like a car show. Agent Lewis and Detective Burns observed from down the street in an unmarked car listening intensely through the recording device. Nita's bad-ass kids ran around like wild animals in the dried up dirt in the front yard where grass use to grow. Her house wasn't worth more than Drape's pinky ring; let alone his gold Presidential Rolex. From the outside, the house was run, but the inside was plush with big screen TV's in every room and leather pit couches. As soon as Drape got out of his car, the football team of kids immediately rushed him.

"Give me some money Uncle Drape!" they yelled simultaneously as they surrounded him. "We know you got pocket full of hundreds."

He reached into his pocket and pulled out his bankroll, peeled off a hundred-dollar bill, and handed it to Nay-Nay, Nita's oldest child. "Split it wit 'dem," Drape said pointing to the rest of the kids.

Nita came out the house and wobbled her fat ass down the front steps over to him. She was straight up ghetto as it gets. With a dingy scarf around her head and no shoes on, she walked toward him on the ball of her heels.

"Give me some money too muthafucka!" she begged. "You won't use my spot for free."

"Here," Drape said peeling off three hundred dollar bills, "I see where 'dem damn kids get dat shit from," he joked.

She released her bright white teeth as she smiled. Nita was fat, but she had the nicest teeth and the prettiest face you've ever seen, accompanied by a great sense of humor. She resembled and had the personality of the comedian, Monique.

"Fuck you, Drape," she shot back, just before they both laughed.

When Drape walked into her house, all of the Scrilla Boys were laid out slothfully over the couches as clouds of marijuana smoke lingered throughout the house. Drape took a seat on the edge of the coffee table in the corner of the living room. He then began to instruct everyone on how they were all going to bring twenty grand apiece to the pot so that they could spend a hundred grand with Shorty. The Feds listened attentively from down the street as he spoke. Tim had already informed them that Shorty wasn't going to holla at Drape because of the incident the night before.

"Why can't you holla at da hoe yo'self?" Romeo uttered being sarcastic with a smile on his face.

"Quit playin' so much. You already know why da hoe ain't fuckin' wit me. Everybody can't be a lady's man like you," Drape shot back. "Besides, aren't you Romeo the pipe-her?"

All the fellas laughed. Soon Romeo did too. He knew his boys had always given him that name because he would hit any bitch with a fat ass any day and lay pipe so good they'd tell the entire hood the following day.

"I'm just fuckin' wit you Drape," Romeo responded.

"Tim, when you tell dat bitch you would call her?" Drape questioned.

"In a couple of days," Tim responded.

"Everybody gon' be ready? I know all y'all mutha-fuckas got big paper. So, can you have it by then?" They all gave a nod.

"Tim, we gone give da money to you so you can handle dat or is dat too much?" Drape continued. "You the only one Shorty really likes." He paused. "hey you fucked my girl?"

"Jokes, huh, real funny ha, ha, ha," Tim replied.

"Make sure y'all ready," Drape repeated and then got up to leave. He grinned like everything was good.

There was no need for him to mention robbing Shorty because Tim already had informed them. Plus he didn't want to give the Feds more than what he had to. Conspiracy to commit murder was a new charge. As the meeting ended they all filed out and hopped into their expensive whips excited about their new deal. Drape was the only one with sadness in his eyes as he thought about what he was doing to his so-called friends. Agent Lewis drove past very slowly as Drape stood on Nita's porch with his hands in his pockes.

"What da fuck was dat all about?" Nita shouted after seeing how Agent Lewis rubbernecked toward her porch. "Who the fuck was dat white bastard?"

"Yo' guess is good as mine." Drape shrugged his shoulders then continued to his car.

Twenty minutes later when Drape turned into the Wal-mart parking lot, Agent Lewis and Detective Burns were sitting on the trunk of Lewis' Ford Taurus smoking a Victory cigarette. Drape pulled up to the rear end where they were sitting and got out nervously handing Agent Lewis the recording device.

"I'll call y'all when we meet up to go get da dope," he

said quickly turning around to go back toward his car.

"We gotta deal for you," Agent Lewis blurted out to get his attention.

Drape stopped dead in his tracks, and turned around. "A deal huh?"

"Give us Shorty and we'll drop all the charges against your brother."

His heart rate increased. The world seemed to come to a stand still. *Shorty is good peoples,* he thought to himself before pulling his cap down. She'd always been there for him when she needed him. But then again…Angel was his blood; the person he was supposed to look out for. Drape's mother counted on him.

"I don't know about dat. I gotta get back wit' y'all," Drape said before hoping back inside his car. He looked back over his shoulder to see Detective Burns burning a hole in his back with fiery eyes. He hated that gruesome keloid on his face. *That nigga* creepy *as shit* he told himself.

Agent Lewis took a long drag off his cigarette then flicked it in the air as he approached Drape's driver side window. He leaned into the window, "Look after we get the Scrilla Boys, I'm sure all of them will write statements on her to get their time cut so don't take too long getting back with me." He exercised his authority and tapped on the side of Drape's door then walking off.

"Fuck!" Drape screamed at the top of his lungs. He had love for Shorty, but his loyalty was to his brother. Blood was blood. However, a bitch was just a bitch. His blood began to boil with anger and frustration. Draped scurried out the parking lot, hoping he wouldn't have to make the wrong move.

CHAPTER 9

Early the next morning Drape received a call from his connect, G-Dolla. That was good news considering G. Dolla was the man in Ohio. He'd acquired a lot of money through the streets of Cleveland because he supplied all the area hustlers with kilos of dope on a daily basis as well as other niggas he'd put in the game.

G-Dolla let him know that the drought was over and that he was back in effect, with a lot of dope to sell. Without even zipping his jeans all the way, Drape raced out of his house excitedly as soon as G Dolla told him to meet him at his sister's house. The ride was short but seemed like a lifetime as Drape thought about his odd situation with Diona and Shorty. Although those were his two favorites girls; there were more, many more. The other chicks in his life meant nothing, nothing more than a fuck. But Drape was tired. He was ready to start a new life, one where he could make legit money and have just one woman.

When he reached G-Dolla's sister's house, he sped in the driveway, parked behind his silver Jaguar, and honked his horn. Within seconds, G-Dolla peeped from the window showing the creases in his forehead. After realizing it was Drape he rushed to open the front door.

"C'mon in, my nigga," he said to Drape as he held the door open then rushed back toward the stove.

G-Dolla's burly body was drenched in sweat as he

stood over the four burner white stove in a black wife beater trying to work his magic. He cooked up the dope in the Pyrex like a pro in front of him. Drape looked on thinking about how his idol was the spitting image of the actor, Idris Elba. He had a muscular physique with a sexy swag. G. Dolla was rugged, yet well respected by many; including drug dealers, people in the community, old folks, and especially the ladies. It always amazed Drape how G. Dolla maintained a laid back personality, never letting his right hand know what his left hand was doing.

"Whassup pimpin'?" G-Dolla asked without taking his eyes off the hot Pyrex as Drape moved to his left side.

"Shit, just takin' it slow. I see we back to business huh?" Drape exclaimed with a smile.

"That's you over there in that blue bag." G-Dolla pointed behind him without breaking his concentration on the dope.

"How much and how many?" Drape asked as he peered inside the bag.

"Ten bricks, fifteen g's a piece. You know the usual."

"I'll hit you when I'm finished."

"Take your time. I got a lot mo shit to move."

"Drape stepped to the door and opened it. "You want me to lock dis bottom lock?"

"Yeah do that. But you know there's not a soul around who's got the balls to come in here and fuck with me." He patted the .45 on his side, then gave Drape a wicked scowl.

Drape nodded, locked the bottom lock and pulled the door shut. *G-Dolla came through just in time,* he thought. He and the Scrilla Boys had planned to cop some dope from Shorty in a couple of days and until now he didn't have it to give to Shorty. As Drape drove off, he picked up his cell phone to call Shorty. Her cell phone rang as he anxiously waited for her to answer.

"What's da business?" Shorty chimed.

"I just seen my connect. Meet me at da Ramada Inn on Bagley Road in Strongsville. Be there in two hours," Drape instructed. He hung up before she could even reply.

Strongsville, Ohio was thirty-five minutes from Cleveland. It was perfect since he didn't want to take any chances on being seen with Shorty. On his way there, he swung by his cook up apartment and dropped off five of the ten bricks he'd just gotten from G-Dolla. The other five bricks he'd give to Shorty, stuffing them into a black duffle bag. He drove extra slow making his way to Strongville, making sure not to get pulled over by the police. By the time Drape arrived at the Ramada Inn and observed Shorty sitting in her Lexus, he felt like he'd done eight hours worth of work as he inched his way beside her car.

Shorty was in chill mode with her elbow resting on the door panel to support her head that lay lazily on her hand. She twirled the gum in her mouth with her index finger as she waited patiently for Drape, the love of her life to show up. Lil' Kim played loudly from her speakers and could be heard from outside the car.

"Hey baby!" she purred as Drape parked on the right hand side of her car.

"Whassup Short Dawg?" he replied as he hopped out.

"Shit, what's up?"

He let out a short sigh, "Tryin' to get a lot of shit done." He breathed heavily as his eyes focused on Shorty's thighs.

Shorty had on a white embellished tank top with some booty shorts exposing her ass of course. Although she was dressed casually, she was sexy as fuck with her long hair pulled up into a ponytail and perfectly applied make-up. She made Drape want to instantly deviate from his plan.

"Here," he tossed the duffle bag into her truck. "It's

five bricks in there. Stash dat until Tim calls you in a few days."

Shorty licked her licks, then raised the volume on her stereo as her favorite verse of Lil' Kim played, "Lie for him, die for him, ruger on the side for him, lift hand high for him." She sang along as she stared at Drape letting him know that's how she felt about him.

Drape smiled as she recited that verse knowing she was truly his ride or die bitch. He puckered his lips to give a kiss from where he sat. She did the same as she slipped her index and middle fingers into her shorts, fingering herself, then pulling them out. She put them in her mouth and sucked on them lustfully, eyeing Drape. She then placed her car in drive.

"You know I'm always gonna be down for you, right?" Shorty commented.

"I know. You got my back. I got yours," Drape lied.

"You mean that, right?" Shorty asked with sincerity.

"Baby, you know I mean it. You shouldn't even ask me no shit like dat," Drape assured.

"Everything okay wit' the Fed situation?"

"For now." He shook his head in frustration.

"A'ight, well call me if you need me." She paused. "Drape, one last thing…would you ever leave Diona for me?" Her eyes softened.

"Shorty, don't do dat! You know how I feel about Diona and you know how I feel about you. I can't have dis conversation right now."

"A'ight, whatever Drape!" Shorty sulked.

"Be careful!" he shouted as she drove off.

He thought about calling Shorty and telling her to turn around, so they could get a room. Then he thought about Diona. He had to try to do the right thing for a change. Drape kept shaking his head as he sat in his car thinking about his life and what he'd become. What would happen when they all found out he was a *SNITCH*?

SNITCH

CHAPTER 10

Hours later Drape ended up stopping by, Angel's crib. He hadn't been spending much time with him since he'd been cooperating with the Feds. At this point, Angel was unaware of the controlled buy the Feds had on him, and Drape had no intentions on letting him know right now. Since they were teenagers, Angel always seemed to leave a mess for Drape to clean up. But for Drape, it never mattered, that was his brother who he cared for dearly.

Drape sounded his horn as he parked in front of Angel's house. Angel glanced out of the window and snatched his jacket off the arm of the chair. He abruptly ran out the house laughing humorously. His front door flung open as he ran toward Drape's car.

"Oh no muthafucka, give me some money!" his baby mamma, Taniqua yelled as Angel jumped in Drape's passenger seat.

"Pull off, pull off!" he shouted to Drape.

"What da fuck!" Drape sped off laughing hysterically at Angel's fast getaway from his crazy, heavy-set baby mamma.

"Big girl gone tear you a new asshole when you get back," Drape teased.

"Money, money, money, that's all she talks about. That bitch know I ain't been fucking with no work since you told me to fall back. She know we been surviving off them two pieces of shit houses. Auntie barely wants to pay me the rent on one of those," Angel commented.

Drape shook his head as he looked at his brother's new jewelry. "You still wanna be a flashy lil' nigga, huh?"

"Just a lil' something," Angel boasted. "Nothing like what you doing. I'm trying to get on your level. But I see you don't fuck with your lil' nigga," Angel joked.

"Naw, I just been tryin' to pull some money together so I can pay those damn lawyers. My connect ain't been havin' shit. My money been funny especially since my crib got hit. A nigga been strugglin' tryin' to put somethin' together. Boy I miss my stick up days."

"You talk to Romeo?" Angel asked.

"Naw, man, why you ask dat?"

"He called me talking about some bitch. I couldn't talk because Taniqua was all down my damn throat."

Drape didn't want Angel hanging with Romeo while the Fed shit was going down. He was already stressing his brain lying to save them both. Drape didn't need him getting in any deeper shit than he was already. His mother would kill him.

Suddenly, Angel's phone rang. "Speak of the devil," he muttered as he looked at his caller I.D. "Whassup lover boy?" he answered.

"Nigga where you at? I just left yo' house," Romeo said in an amplified tone.

"I'm in the car with Drape."

"Tell dat nigga I said whassup."

"Romeo said whassup," Angel said to Drape.

"Tell dat nigga I said whassup and don't be tryin' to get you in no bullshit."

"He said whassup," Angel said to Romeo leaving out the rest of Drape's reply.

"Romeo said, where we about to go?" Angel added.

Drape lowered the volume a notch on his ride, "Some-where yo' ass ain't," he joked, "Naw, I'm just fuckin' wit you. We on our way up to *Strictly Business*," shouting loud enough for Romeo to hear.

Strictly Business was a detail shop where anybody who had a nice car sitting pretty went to get their car washed.

"I'll meet y'all up there," Romeo insisted.

"A'ight," Angel said ending the call.

In less than a half hour later Drape could see Romeo's long-limbed six foot figure standing in front of his cranberry colored BMW 750LI, flagging him down as they neared the detailed shop. Romeo's bald head shone as he tried to play mack daddy on some chick who'd just gotten her car cleaned. It was also clear from her giggles and schoolgirl behavior that she liked what Romeo was saying. It was clear that Romeo was known as a ladies man and had a reputation for having a big dick throughout the hood.

"Look at dis nigga!" Drape commented turning into the lot. "Dat crazy muthafucka must've flown up here and now he already scoutin' pussy," Drape said to Angel, before they both laughed.

Drape pulled his car in front of *Strictly Business*, and hopped out like he was the man. He tossed his keys with per-fection to the young boy who washed the cars. "Pull it in," he stated to the young boy.

"Me," the young boy replied, pointing to himself. He was astonished to be asked to pull Drape's Benz inside the wash area.

"Yeah you," Drape remarked. "And take good care of her too," he boasted.

Drape, Angel, and Romeo took a seat on a dingy back seat that used to be on a bus. Before Drape could even sit down, Romeo was putting in his plea.

"I gotta lick fo' us landin' us about a hundred g's. I

know we said we wasn't gone hit licks no more but dis one is sweeeeeeeeeet," Romeo sang.

"On who?" Drape asked curiously.

"Dis hoe I be fuckin' got a baby daddy named Jamaican Dee from da Rock."

The Rock was short for the Rocky River projects on the west side of Cleveland. A place where most even hated to visit. Jamaican Dee was well known in that area and also known for killing a lot of people. Drape had met him only once, remembering that he wasn't easy on the eyes. He was dark as tar with long dreadlocks to the middle of his back and had daunting dark beady eyes that pierced anyone he looked at.

Rumor had it that the scar on the left side of Jamaican Dee's face would put one in the mind of Freddy Krueger. At 6'2, and a hundred and seventy-five pounds, Jamaican Dee's reputation was clear- he wasn't to be fucked with. Drape knew that if they robbed Jamaican Dee, there would be repercussions if he found out. The way things were going, he had enough problems to deal with.

"And why would a bitch set her baby father up for you?" Drape asked with a serious expression.

"'Cause the nigga doin' her dirty. He makin' all the money and won't give her none. Baby girl even said her child support less than food stamp money. I guess she on get back, or maybe it's because the nigga got a little dick." Romeo laughed wildly as he grabbed at his own dick.

"Hell nah, leave dat shit alone," Drape said firmly. He got up off the seat just as Romeo's car was being pulled around. Angel followed his brother toward the wash area as Romeo pleaded.

"C'mon man!" Romeo said standing up.

Angel stopped and turned back toward Romeo and put his hand up to his mouth like a phone. "Call me," he mouthed without making a sound.

Romeo winked then walked to his car that shined from the roof to the wheels. He passed off a twenty dollar tip loving the fact that he was thought of as a big shot.

Drape watched Romeo speed off as the young boy pulled his Benz to the front shine area. While he and Angel waited for the young boy to put the finishing touches on the car, the young boy and the other employees cleaned Drape's car inside by taking the mats out, discarding trash, and vacuuming the carpet. The windows were windexed to perfection and the vanilla scented air freshener was sprayed inside just before Drape stepped back inside.

By the time everything was complete, Drape's white 500SL seemed to glow right along with his twenty inch Lowenhart rims that shined to perfection. He smiled as he handed the young boy a crisp fifty dollar bill.

"Keep da change," Drape bragged.

SNITCH

CHAPTER 11

After cruising through the hoods for a while, Drape decided to stop by Monroe's Strip Joint, the club where Porsha danced to have a few drinks. As soon as he and Angel strutted through the double doors, the eyes of all the strippers followed them like a lion stalking its prey. Not only was Drape known for being a baller, but they both had on enough jewelry to light up the entire club. Angel took a seat at a table as he approached the bar.

"Give me a double Remy and a double Grey Goose with Hypnotic," Drape said to the bartender as he peeled some dollars off his bankroll.

"You want a dance?" a stripper asked standing next to him.

Drape knew what time it was as the stripper never took her eyes off his cash. "Out of all da times you seen me in here, you ain't never seen me get a lap dance, but you know what, you can give him one," he instructed. Drape pointed to Angel, then stuffed a twenty in the tap around her thigh.

He felt lap dances were for perverts. When he came to the strip club, it was to watch the stage only. Besides he'd fucked damn near every stripper in the club already. When the stripper approached Angel, his attention was on the stage. He was caught off guard when she stood in between his legs, pushing them open, using hers. She tooted her nice shaped apple ass in his face and began to rotate it Reggae style.

Angel instantly blushed as he turned and looked at Drape who sat at the bar snickering.

"Ecstasy to the stage, Ecstasy to the stage," the D.J. announced.

Out of the blue, a tall caramel stallion with two big braids hanging from both sides of her head strutted toward the stage. Ecstasy put you in mind of Pocahontas, but with the body of the rapper Trina and a slightly lighter skin tone. Her walk was hard and confident letting everyone know that she was a bad bitch.

"Damn," Drape mumbled to himself. He then motioned anxiously for Porsha to come over to where he sat. Porsha was in the middle of running game on an older white man when she noticed Drape's annoying hand signals. Her sigh showed that she didn't appreciate being interrupted.

"I'll be right back baby," she said softly to the white man, then swung her blond wig to the left.

Porsha waltzed over to Drape and asked, "What boy, I'm working!"

"Who dat?" Drape pointed to the stage with lust filled eyes.

"Dat's Ecstasy."

"Who?" Drape inquired again.

"Ecstasy. She from da Rock. Dat's Jamaican Dee's baby mamma. Look, Shorty wouldn't like us havin' dis conversation. Plus, she be fuckin' wit Romeo so don't ask me to do it," Porsha said hurrying back over to the white guy before another stripper made their move on him.

"Ohhhhhhh," Drape mumbled remembering what Romeo said earlier at *Strictly Business*.

Angel walked up to the bar only to find his brother in deep thought. "Muthafucka you sicked that chick on me huh?"

Drape couldn't even respond. The sound of David

Banner's *"Like A Pimp,"* throbbed through the speakers as Ecstasy squatted and started to make her ass cheeks clap to the beat while gripping the pole. From where Drape sat, he was able to get a full view of her plump ass. While both men sat in amazement, Ecstasy dropped down to the floor and reared back showing her closely shaven pussy.

Angel shouted like he was at a concert. "Got damn, Ecstasy…Got Damn!" Drape and Angel made eye contact simultaneously. "Damn she thick!" Angel exclaimed. He was mesmerized by all the ass she carried around.

Drape just shook his head and told himself, "Romeo better watch himself." Before long the show was over and Drape ordered another round as he stood and dropped a fifty on the countertop for the barmaid. "Meet me in the car," he told Angel as he walked toward the door. Drape stopped and turned to get one last look at Ecstasy making sure she saw him too.

Once in the car, Drape and Angel fantasized about what they would both do to Ecstasy if given the chance as they flew down Interstate 90. It was all jokes and laughs until Drape noticed that a black Chrysler had been making every turn he did and was now following three yards behind. At first, he assumed it was the Feds. Then after making a sharp left unexpectedly, he realized it was a young boy, late teens at the most. Who? He didn't know.

SNITCH

CHAPTER 12

Diona pulled up to their Moreland Hills home and pulled directly into the garage. Drape wasn't home yet, which was cool with her because she wanted to relax for a little before her man showed up at the house. When Diona walked through the side door of the garage and into the kitchen, she sat down on the bar stool hoping for a quick break. She hadn't even taken her bags out of the car yet, because there was so much stuff to load into the house from shopping.

Instantly, Diona thought about the mail. She hopped up, holding her stomach, and rushed to the front door, grabbing the mail off the floor that had been delivered through the mail chute. All her favorite magazines were scattered about; Black Enterprise, Essence, and her favorite, the Parenthood Magazine. Of course there were bills too, and strangely an envelope addressed to Diona Young without a return address. Without hesitation, Diona began to open the envelope as she walked back toward the garage to get her bags. Enclosed was a letter, which read:

Diona,
My name is Stacy. First of all, I'm not crazy, I just wanted to inform you that Drape is a piece of shit. I'm the woman who Drape's been with for the past four months if you didn't know. When I met him, he told me that he didn't have anyone and he was single until someone told me about you the other day. He never told me about his expecting a baby. I

met his brother, Angel and the Scrilla Boys, vice versa. I get the dick on the regular, so that's why I never thought that he had a girl. I felt I needed to contact you and let you know because since he played me, I want you to feel the same. I'm not into sharing men, but Drape always made it seem like he was single. I wanted to let you know what "our" man was up to. I hear you're an uppity bitch, so I give Drape what you obviously can't. I wish you and Drape the best of luck with your future and I hope this letter was helpful to you. I also enclosed a picture so that you would know that I'm telling the truth. If you need a shoulder to cry on, call me at 216-304-5555 after you're done going crazy. Smoochies! P.S. I'm not the only one either, check that bitch, Shorty!

Diona gasped for air. For her it was certain that she wouldn't be able to breathe much longer. Her hands began to feel clammy and beads of sweat formed on top of her head. She stumbled slightly, feeling faint, and a sour taste developed in her mouth. Diona tried to make it back to the kitchen to catch her balance on the granite countertop, but she vomited all over the floor. The thought of Drape fucking a random bitch made her feel dizzy. Diona's mind flashed to the photo. The bitch in the picture looked like a trashy stripper. So many emotions raced through her.

At that moment, Diona grabbed the cordless phone. It was time to talk to Shorty face-to-face. Anger filled every bone as she dialed Shorty's number. Diona leaned on the counter and began to cry profusely as the ringing sound began. Suddenly, Diona stood, sucked up the tears and hung up.

"I can't do this anymore!" Diona cried out as she flung the cordless phone across the room violently, hitting the wall. The battery instantly flew from the back. "How the fuck did this crazy bitch get my address and know my full name?" she asked herself. "What type of bitches does this dumb ass nigga fuck with? Trifling son a bitch!"

Diona knelt down to the floor and crossed her legs like a lonely toddler. She needed someone to confide in. Someone to tell her Drape was some shit. Someone to tell her to leave Drape for good.

She always suspected Drape of fucking around, but knowing her address was a bit much. Diona knew this crazy bitch was trying to hurt her, not Drape. And the fact that another woman could confirm her suspicions about Shorty sent Diona into a crying marathon. She sat sobbing in the middle of the floor wondering, why.

"All the lies. All the damn lies," she cried.

She couldn't help but think about his family and friends always lying for him, and Drape trying to convince her that she was the crazy one.

"Calm down Diona, calm down Diona," she kept saying to herself. She needed to pull herself together. She didn't want to inform Drape yet, however it was going to be difficult trying to hide it. Her insides were raging with hurt and anger. The mere thought of his sorry ass made her nauseous all over again.

"Why do these hoes think that they can take a man from his family? If he can fuck a bitch on the side, why upgrade the hoe?" Diona acted like she was in a psychiatric asylum having a conversation with herself. "This bitch is crazy if she think she's gonna fuck my man and create havoc within my household!" She yelled erratically and pointed as if someone were in front of her.

"What part of the game is this where a bitch sends me a letter? This broad is lucky I'm pregnant, or I would beat the breaks off this hoe and Shorty." Diona continued to rant and rave. She yelled like a mad woman, still talking to herself. "Pay back is a bitch. This nigga really thinks he's gonna get away with this, and I'm pregnant, hell nah! Where they do that at?"

Diona got up from the floor and went to her truck in the garage to get her cell phone. She needed to make a call and gain some clarification on the situation. She knew she could call one person who would keep it real. The one person who knew a lot about Drape. The one person Drape would flip on if he knew Diona had called him.

The phone rang twice.

"Hello," the unknown person answered quickly.

"Hey, it's me Diona! I need to ask you something and I want you to keep it one hundred percent with me."

"Sure. Is somethin' wrong wit' the baby? Where's Drape?"

"The baby is fine," she muttered with a shaky voice. "And I don't know where Drape is, I just got home. Listen, I came home from shopping and there was a letter from some girl saying that she fucks with Drape and that he also fucks with Shorty. She even had the nerve to send a picture," Diona explained in a frenzy.

"Look Diona, first calm down! You know I never get in Drape's business when it comes to you, but you can't keep lettin' him play you for a fool. Yeah, he loves you, but you deserve better! Who sent the letter, Stacy?"

"Yeah, how did you know? You met her and didn't tell me, huh?"

"Diona, if Drape knew that we talked, it would be beef, trust me! Listen the Stacy bitch is a hoe, she fucks wit' everybody. I'm not tryin' to hate on Drape or take up for him, but dis is crazy. No one is perfect, but regardless of what bitch he fucks with, she should never disrespect you like dat. Drape does love you. He just doesn't realize that anotha' nigga would be happy to be in his shoes right now!"

Diona allowed a few tears to escape even after she promised herself that she wouldn't cry on the phone. "It just hurts so badly that he would do this to me. I've been here through thick and thin and he fucking Shorty under my nose." Diona sobbed uncontrollably.

"Wow! Diona there's alot goin' on, but I know the Shorty shit is fucked up too. Drape is a nigga, like I'm a nigga, you just have to do what's best fo' you and yo' seed. Did you tell Drape about da letter yet?"

"No, you're the only one who knows! Don't mention it to anyone. I don't want it getting back to Drape yet."

"You have my word. You need anything? Do you want to go somewhere and clear your mind?" The unknown person asked.

"Yeah, I feel like my heart is in a thousand pieces. I can't face Drape right now! I need to think," Diona cried.

"A'ight, I'll make arrangements for you to stay at Walden in Aurora. It's an exclusive spa and you can stay there and rest for however long you need. It's on me. If you need anything else, just call me."

"You don't have to pay for it, I have it."

"Naw, I insist! Get you and the baby some rest. I'll call later and make sure you made it."

"Thanks! I owe you!" Diona said sounding a little more together.

"No, just think and decide what you wanna do. You not wrong if you leave and you not stupid for stayin'. Do you!" the unknown person encouraged.

Deep inside, the caller was glad that Drape had fucked up. He was going to play it cool hoping to one day get Diona for himself. He always had a thing for Diona and envied Drape because of her. He would do anything for her and she didn't even know it. Unfortunately, Diona only saw him as a friend. Diona was all for Drape, yet he knew it would have been only a matter of time she would find out about Stacy or Shorty.

"Alright Bye!" Diona said hanging up.

Diona went upstairs to her bedroom with the letter in her hand. She kept a lockbox hidden in her closet from Drape that contained money she'd been stacking. She kept the money "just in case" some bullshit like this happened. After shaking her head one last time, Diona opened the lockbox and folded the letter, putting it inside. She then got out her Louis Vuitton Duffle bag and threw three days worth of clothes inside. She also threw a couple stacks of money in the bag as well. Whatever she didn't have, she would buy. Diona then put the lockbox safely back to where it was hidden, leaving out of her closet.

Going back downstairs, Diona cleaned the vomit off the floor and picked up the broken cordless phone. She didn't want Drape to notice anything unusual. She then threw her bag in her truck, and whipped her ride out the garage. Diona turned her cell phone off just in case Drape tried to call and proceeded to Walden for some much needed "me" time. She wanted Drape to feel the pain of not knowing where she was, just as he'd done to her on several occasions.

"Muthafucka!" Diona chanted to herself.

CHAPTER 13

Romeo pulled up slowly in front of Monroe's just before closing, headed to pick up Ecstasy. Realizing that Tim's Lexus was sitting in front of him, Romeo pulled up as close as he could trying to piss his friend off. The lights from Romeo's BMW reflected off his rearview and into Tim's eyes causing him to sit up in the seat. After hitting the lights, Romeo got out and approached the car. Tim hit his unlock button as he got closer.

"Whassup?" Romeo asked as he got in the passenger seat.

"Waitin' on dis hoe to come out," Tim replied angrily while trying to hold his blunt. "Nigga you ever heard of low beams?"

Romeo laughed to himself. "Nigga, you always complainin'. How long you been waitin'?"

"Too fuckin' long. But I'm sure you'll wait as long as you need to, just to fuck Ecstasy. I know dat hoe got some good, fat, wet pussy." Tim paused then took another puff. "I can tell by da way she walk!" He laughed for half a second then changed his demeanor to a more serious look. "You know they say dat hoe scandalous?" His expression told his boy that Ecstasy could mean trouble.

"Who told you dat bullshit, let me guess, Porsha gossipin' ass. Nigga y'all made fo' each other. Pillow talkin' muthafuckas," Romeo said with an evil look.

"You damn right! My hoe better let me know about a bitch when she fuckin' wit' one of my niggas, ya feel me?" Tim grumbled as he stuck his fist out for dap. Romeo smiled as he gave Tim dap knowing he meant nothing but good.

A few seconds later, the club doors opened and Porsha and Ecstasy walked out giggling. Porsha strutted up to Tim's passenger door and tugged on the handle. Strangely, she wasn't wearing her favorite blonde wig. Her natural beauty showed with her short, natural, shaved haircut.

"Open da door," she barked while Romeo cracked a smile and pointed to the backseat. She instantly threw a tantrum stomping her feet as she pouted. "Come on boy stop fuckin' playin'. I been on my feet all damn day," she whined with her face sulking.

Ecstasy blushed as she stood behind Porsha seductively with her arms crossed. "So, are you gonna sit there and play games, or are we gonna get outta here?" She licked her lips lustfully and eyeballed Romeo's dick print in his jeans.

Romeo opened the door and began to rise slowly out the seat pretending like her words didn't affect him. "I'm bout to fuck da shit out of dis' bitch," he whispered to Tim as he got up out the seat.

Porsha impatiently yanked him by his shoulder, then slid her body into the passenger seat. "I'll see you tomorrow girl," she said to Ecstasy while Tim placed the car in drive.

"What took you so long?" Romeo kidded with Ecstasy as they got inside his car.

"Don't even try it, I saw you on the camera when you pulled up," she informed. "You just got here."

Ecstasy immediately got freaky as she heard R. Kelly singing, *"Seems Like You're Ready,"* playing through the sound system in the car. Before Romeo could get the gear shift out of park, she was fondling his huge dick through his pants. "I wanna fuck right now," she taunted while pressing her hand forcefully against his hardness. Ecstasy moved her body seductively around in the seat and rubbed one leg against the other as if her pussy were on fire.

"C'mon girl. What's up wit da move on yo' baby father?" he asked jerking away from her hot tongue that had made its way into his ear and down to the side of his neck. Romeo hated whenever his tattoo was touched.

"I told you he's coming through tonight baby," Ectasy replied as she continued to fondle him.

"What time?"

"About four o' clock in the morning," she said, unzipping his pants.

Romeo turned sharply as he turned onto West 25th Avenue but Ecstasy didn't care. She had her mind set on Romeo's dick. Romeo may have been a cocky muthafucka but she knew that he knew how to lay the pipe so whatever it took to make him happy would get done. Ecstasy leaned over the middle console of the Lexus into Romeo's lap. Taking his hardened pipe out, she admired it like the world's best treasure. She then gently massaged it, looking seductively at Romeo while licking her lips. Swiftly, Ecstasy got on all fours as the car swerved to get in a more comfortable position.Her goal was to properly serve him. She was bent over with her knees grounded in the passenger seat and her ass rotated in the air. At that moment, Ecstasy spit on his infamous magic stick until her saliva rushed down his pole, lubricating it. She stroked it with her left hand as she sucked on his sensitive head.

"Oh shit." Romeo gyrated in his seat as he veered slightly off the road.

She deep throated his whole anaconda in her mouth, while licking his shaft with her tongue. With every lick, she became even more horny. The more she licked, the more she wanted his love stick in her wet, juicy canal.

"Oh shit, Ecstasy, damn!" he moaned, grasping the back of her head, and letting the wheel go completely. The car stopped in the middle of the road like a disabled vehicle as cars passing blew their horns disrespectfully.

"Wait muthafuckas," Romeo tried to shout. His head was thrown all the way back and his mouth was wide open.

As Ecstasy tried to suck the life out him, she took her right hand and put it in between her legs. Rubbing on her bare waxed pussy, it wasn't long before her slim fingers made their way to her clit. Ecstasy's pussy began to tingle. Romeo became more aroused as he watched Ecstasy play with herself and suck him off at the same time.

"Damn, you a bad bitch! Shiiiitttttt! Romeo groaned. "Take all dis nut," he blurted out.

Ecstasy continued to slurp until he blasted his baby batter into her mouth. She swallowed every last drop while making her panties drenched with her pussy juices.

"Yo, we need to go. I'ma drop you off at da house, then go get my nigga," Romeo said trying to regain his normal breathing pattern.

"Oh no, don't go get him until we fuck," Ecstasy pleaded.

Romeo put the car in drive thinking about how good a fuck Ecstasy was. Her head game was so bomb that he'd even taken her to his crib before. "Damn," he kept repeating as he drove.

"Look, I wanna fuck when we get to my house," Ecstasy said as she sat back in the seat then flipped the visor down. Looking into the mirror, she patted her hair into place and dabbed a cloth at the sides of her mouth.

"We ain't got enough time. It's two in da mornin'. But I'll be right back as soon as I get my man," Romeo replied.

"How looong!" she whined.

"Twenty minutes," he said pulling up in her driveway.

Not trying to be a bitch, Ecstasy got out, unlocked her front door, then walked back up to the passenger side window. "Here, take my keys just in case I'm asleep when you get back. This is my only key so don't lose it. I can't lock my door without it," she said trying to be slick. "Hurry up baby!"

"Bet," Romeo said as he pulled off.

He called Angel letting him know he was on the way. Angel knew he shouldn't have planned to do the robbery after Drape told him and Romeo to leave it alone, but he felt like he needed to make his own money for a change. Romeo hit his lights as he pulled into Angel's driveway. Angel came walking out of his back yard dressed in all black and a bold expression on his face that said he was ready to put in work. On the way back to Ecstasy's house, Romeo gave Angel the rundown on how they were going to pull off the stick-up.

Jamaican Dee was driving from Columbus, which was two hours away from Cleveland. From what Ecstasy had told him, he was in Columbus hustling with some niggas he'd met at the Columbus block party from 18th and Long Street. Every week he drove from Columbus to Ecstasy's house alone to count his money before he dropped it off at his stash spot, before going back. Ecstasy had set it up perfectly.

Romeo slowed down as he pulled into the Shaker Heights area. He passed her house seeing if Jamaican Dee's Tahoe was in the driveway. When there was no sight of the SUV, Romeo continued down the street until he came to a dark spot and parked. Together, they discreetly walked toward Ecstasy's house re-playing in their heads how things would go.

Ecstasy rented a two-bedroom home that was part of a two family in Shaker Heights on Daleford Avenue. It was a very diverse suburb where people lived on Section-8, to home owners living in colonial mansions. Ecstasy resided downstairs, the unit facing the street. Luckily, the landlord hadn't rented the upstairs yet. Her late night rendezvous would've driven most neighbors living that close crazy anyway.

Ecstasy was in her bedroom when she heard Angel and Romeo come into the house. Romeo grabbed the remote control off the arm of the couch and turned on the T.V. tossing it to Angel. Angel felt comfortable immediately. Ecstasy's home had an eclectic vibe to it with incense and candles burning all around. She also had naked pictures of beautiful African people on her wall and wood carved statues of exotic animals throughout her living and dining room. Her home welcomed anyone with a warm and cozy feel.

Romeo grinned at Angel as he walked toward her bedroom. "Nigga, don't beat your dick when you hear all this good fuckin' goin' on."

Angel laughed then took a seat on the couch as Romeo walked toward Ecstasy's room. At the same time, they both heard her phone ringing. Romeo had walked in just in time to see Ecstasy win her Academy Award.

"Hello," she answered groggily as if she was asleep.

Ecstasy was grimey by nature, and Jamaican Dee knew it. She had entitlement issues where she felt Jamaican Dee should've given her more money monthly than what he actually did. The fact that Dee would use her spot to count thousands in front of her then say he didn't have any money when Ecstasy would ask, pissed her off. It was crazy how they had a child together that he rarely saw and rarely provided for; except for the monthly $500 cash child support payment that he'd leave on the kitchen table.

So for Ecstasy, she didn't mind setting him up because she was going to get some money out of the deal and the best dick in town from Romeo. Romeo made her feel good when she was around him and sexed her far better than Dee ever could.

"Hey, me talkin' to ya. Wake up! Me be dere' in forty-five minutes, Kim don't be sleep," Jamaican Dee said as he sped down the highway. He refused to call her by her stage name, especially since they'd been together way before she started stripping.

"A'ight," she replied then hung up.

"Who was dat?" Romeo asked standing in the doorway.

"That was him. He's on his way, so he'll be here in forty-five minutes."

"Dat's what I'm talkin' bout!" Romeo exclaimed.

Ecstasy hung up the phone and motioned for Romeo to approach the bed where she laid ready for action. "Gimme some of that good dick real quick," she told him unzipping his pants as he stood perspiring next to the bed. Ecstasy wasted no time as she leaned over and stuffed Romeo's stiff meat deep into her mouth. Quickly, Romeo began to fuck her mouth with fast thrusts, moving his dick back and forth. He moaned as a little of his nectar squirted into Ecstasy's mouth and she swallowed with a massive gulp. Romeo wasn't ready to cum yet so he pulled out.

"Turn around, I want that ass from back," he demanded.

Ecstasy obliged and tooted her ass so far in the air that her chest was flat on the bed. Her arms were sprawled out holding onto the mattress. "Fuck me, daddy! Beat this pussy up!" she chanted.

Romeo inserted his love cane into her juicy canal and began to plunge in and out. Slow at first, then quickly picked up the pace.

"Ahh shit! Ohh shit!" Ecstasy yelled.

"Uhhhhh shit!" Romeo shouted as he fucked harder like a porno star on set.

"That's my spot, baby! That's my spot!"

"Fuck! This shit is good!" Romeo panted.

"Fuck- fuck- me- in my ass!" Ecstasy insisted, between breaths.

"You sure? You want this dick in yo' ass?" Romeo questioned as he slapped her right cheek.

"Yes baby, give it to me!"

Romeo took his middle finger and thrust it into her asshole, pressing in and out. Wanting it nice and wet, he inserted his long pipe into her ass and began to fuck it like a pro. Moments later, Romeo grabbed her hips with his hands and pulled her ass back and forth on his dick.

"Ahhhhh!" Ecstasy yelled. "Don't stop, that shit feels gooooooooood."

"I'm 'bout to cum!" Romeo bellowed as he grabbed her butt cheeks, gradually sliding partly out of her ass so that he could see his milky liquid squirt into her butt cavity.

"Shit!" Ecstasy said in a daze as she rolled off her stomach, onto her back. After catching her breath, she threw on her robe and ran to use the bathroom to wash herself up. She then brought a washcloth back for Romeo to wipe his dick off.

"So look, bionic dick…let's talk business," she said to Romeo as he cleaned himself up.

Romeo put his pants on, ignoring Ecstasy as he walked into the living room with her in tow.

"Nigga don't be on no bullshit and I better be able to get in touch with your ass after tonight," she said in a sassy tone. She stood in the doorway to the living room with one hand on her hip and the other supporting her as she leaned against the door frame.

"Don't even try and play me like dat," Romeo shot back. "Let's roll, Dee on his way," he said to Angel.

Ecstasy stared intensively at Angel as he rose up off the couch. "Fix my damn pillows," she roared. Ecstasy had a very well-kept house. It was neat without any clutter. Her family always said she had obsessive compulsive disorder when it came to cleaning. She couldn't focus when things were out of place. With her working a strip club, she always disinfected behind some of the girls and kept this routine at home. Angel avoided eye contact as he followed Romeo out the door. *Where da hell did I see dat nigga from*, she thought.

SNITCH

Angel and Romeo waited patiently behind a bush for Jamaican Dee to pull up into Ecstasy's backyard. She'd told them everything they needed to know about his routine. Finally, after about fifteen minutes, the lights from his Tahoe reflected off the garage door as he pulled in the driveway. Jamaican Dee hopped out of his truck with his normal arrogant walk and carrying a large, green trash bag. As he approached the back door his dreadlocks remained firmly tied up in a bun by a sturdy rubberband.

Angel quickly jumped like a renegade from behind the large bush where they hid and softly pressed his forty caliber up to the back of Jamaican Dee's neck. He took a firm hold of the collar of his shirt to make sure he didn't attempt to run.

"You know what it is, lay the fuck down!" Angel demanded through clenched teeth as he forced him face first to the pavement.

"C'mon don't do dis ta me," Jamaican Dee pleaded, catching a glimpse of the tattoo on Romeo's neck.

"Shut da fuck up!" Romeo barked and then snatched the hefty bag of money from his hand.

Jamaican Dee glanced toward Ecstasy's window, noticing her slightly peeking through the cracked blinds. He hoped she would call the police, but something deep down inside told him that she wouldn't.

"Let's go," Romeo uttered.

Angel wouldn't move. Hate filled his eyes as he stood over Jamaican Dee with his gun pointed at his back.

"Let's go," Romeo repeated.

Angel glanced at Romeo then let off two shots into Jamaican Dee's back.

"What da fuck, man? That wasn't supposed to happen!" Romeo shouted in a panic.

Jamaican Dee squirmed and groaned in pain, while Angel stood frozen. Angel didn't want to take any chances on him retaliating so he let off another shot to make sure he would die. Romeo took off running, sweating profusely, wondering why the fuck Angel had complicated things.

When Angel and Romeo finally made it back to Romeo's car, they were both gasping for breath. "Damn, why you shoot da nigga? We had da money!" Romeo whined as he sped off, "I think dat nigga dead," he continued.

"You damn right he's dead," Angel commented trying to play tough. Romeo just looked at his boy's baby brother wondering what he'd gotten them into.

Angels' next comment shocked Romeo even more."We should double back and kill that bitch. She might go to the police."

Romeo banged his fist on the dash. "No! Let me handle her!" Romeo shot Angel a mean mug. "You just betta hope he dead!"

All Angel could think was that he'd fucked up this time and that he should've listened to Drape. He felt Ecstasy was going to fuck up some way or somehow.

CHAPTER 14

Romeo's cell phone rang as he slept on Angel's living room couch. Thinking it might be important, he quickly jumped up and answered.

"Hello," he answered in an antsy tone.

"Why the fuck did y'all shoot him?" Ecstasy screamed.

"Hold da fuck up! Who da fuck you screamin' at?"

"I'm just saying, I didn't want y'all to shoot 'em," she exclaimed.

Deep inside, Romeo wished like hell Angel hadn't pulled that stunt. "Is he dead?" he asked hesitantly.

"No, he's not dead. He's in critical condition at Metro Hospital."

A lump instantly formed in his throat. He knew somehow his boys would be on some retaliation shit. Things were getting crazy so he knew he'd have to watch his back.

"I just left the hospital sitting with him," Ecstasy whimpered. "Some detectives grilled the shit out of me, and Dee kept giving me suspicious looks."

"What they ask?" Romeo covered the phone as Angel walked into the room. He gave Angel a sign that Ecstasy was on the phone.

"They asked if I saw anything, or if I had a clue who would want him dead."

"What you say? Did they believe you?" Romeo asked

giving her the third degree.

"Look I didn't tell them shit," she sighed tired of his, interrogation.

"I got da money. We gon' split it like we said. I'll call you in a couple days after shit die down. Is dat cool?"

"Yeah be careful, I love you," she uttered softly.

Romeo turned and looked at Angel who now sat beside him, staring down his throat. He cracked a smile as he told Ecstasy he loved her back then hung up. Angel was anxious to hear what he had to say.

"What did that bitch say?"

"She said he in critical condition," Romeo announced.

"Damn!" Angel shouted in disappointment. He got up and began to pace back and forth. Now he really regretted not killing Ecstasy.

"Something's gotta be done about her," Angel mumbled to himself. "I already know Drape's gonna call your ass and flip the fuck out when he hear about what happened to Jamaican Dee. You better make sure that hoe doesn't tell Porsha's gossiping ass!" Angel continued.

"One thing I can say about her is dat she know how to keep her mouth shut," Romeo said with confidence. "Lemme' get to da house," he grumbled, grabbing the bag containing the hundred grand in it. The plan was to share it with Ecstasy giving her twenty grand and keeping eighty grand for him and Angel to split.

"Can I get my money now before shit go sour. I might have to leave town."

"Calm da fuck down!" Romeo suggested as he shook his head and smiled at Angel's paranoid ass. "Let me count it all first, then we'll split it."

At that moment, Angel's baby momma, Taniqua overhead their conversation and came into the room. "What y'all talking about?"

SNITCH

Drape laid on his favorite recliner with his phone on his lap hoping Diona would call. It had been one full night, the first time that she'd ever stayed away from home. He'd left twenty-two messages exactly, but none got returned. *Had Diona left him for good*? he wondered. Suddenly his phone rang.

"What's da business?" Drape answered anxiously.

"Dawg, I know you heard what happened to dat nigga Jamaican Dee last night," Tim sputtered.

"Naw, what happened?" Drape already had a bad feeling. He had a good idea about what had happened and by whom.

"Somebody shot dat nigga up over his baby mamma's house."

"He dead?" Drape asked. He knew that if he wasn't dead, Romeo had problems coming his way. He had no clue that Angel was involved.

"Naw, he in critical condition."

"Don't Romeo be fuckin' his baby mamma?" Drape inquired, just trying to analyze Tim's reply.

"Yeah, I seen him last night outside da strip club waitin' on her to get off. Porsha called Ecstasy dis mornin' while she was at da hospital. She said Romeo dropped her off last night and kept it movin'."

"Oh, her and Porsha be kickin' it?"

"Yeah they on some buddy-buddy shit," Tim retorted.

"Lemme' hit you back," Drape said rushing off the phone. He didn't want to get deep in the conversation and ignite Tim's suspicion of Romeo's involvement. He immediately hung up and called Romeo.

"Where da fuck you at?" Drape shouted as soon as

Romeo answered.

"At my momma's house, why what's up?" he said calmly.

"Don't go no fuckin' where, I'm on my way."

"What's wrong?" Romeo asked playing stupid.

"C'mon, don't play dat stupid. Roll wit' me nigga."

-CLICK-

Drape tried Diona again, but every time he called, it went straight to voicemail. After waiting a few seconds, Drape called her phone again just to listen to her voice on the message. He didn't know what the hell was going on. This was unlike her to just disappear. All he knew was that her favorite overnight bag and toothbrush were both gone. He couldn't call her family because they would probably have a victory party.

"Diona, please call me and lemme know if you okay!" he begged. "You carryin' my seed, and I need to know where you are. What did I do? I love you baby." He spoke to Diona's voicemail as if she was listening on the other end.

After slipping on a pair of jeans and a plain white t-shirt, Drape left out the house and jumped in his car. He couldn't sit at home waiting for Diona anymore and he needed to see what was up with Romeo. He was becoming enraged. All he could think about as he drove was the amount of bad luck he was having. When he pulled up to Romeo's mother's house, Romeo was sitting in his BMW in the driveway.

He could see Drape's angry facial expression and wondered if he'd found out that Angel was involved. Drape got out of his car, leaned up against the hood of his Honda and waved for Romeo to come over to where he stood. His arms were crossed across his chest as his face sulked. Like an obedient child, Romeo got out of his car and approached him.

"What da fuck is goin' on?" Drape angrily asked.

"What you talkin' about?"

"I'm talkin' about Jamaican Dee muthafucka! C'mon nigga you just asked me to hit da lick wit' you."

Romeo thought for a second, "Fuck it, I did da shit," he said as he threw his hands up.

Drape shook in head in disappointment, "You know it's gone be some shit behind dat," he grumbled. He held his hand out cutting Romeo off from uttering excuses, "You don't realize that yo' stupid moves could bring heat to all of us." Before Romeo could respond, Drape continued. "Just be at Nita's house in two hours. We got other business to handle," he said, hopping back in the car.

Drape decided not to waste anymore time bitching at Romeo any longer because the damage had already been done. He understood old habits were hard to break. Although he wasn't in charge of Romeo, he was still the one all the fellas looked up to. Most times he carried the weight for them all. Drape dialed up Shorty as he drove off in a rage. Everything seemed to be crumbling in his life.

"Shorty," he barked abruptly when she answered.

Shorty seemed a little standoffish and didn't give Drape the normal greeting he was used to. "What's up?"

"I got problems."

"Oh," she answered making sure she kept things short with Drape.

"Look, I'm not sure why you in a funk, but just know that Tim will be callin' later for those five bricks." He stopped abruptly. "Oh…and remind me to go get that cash from under the porch. 1425, "he said firmly, as if Shorty was some sort of secretary.

"Gotcha," Shorty said making sure she stuck with one-word replies. Then out of the blue, she asked, "You heard about Jamaican Dee getting shot?"

"Naw, I didn't hear. But I gotta go. I'll holla at you

later," Drape informed as he rolled up on Diona's parent's block. He'd hoped to find her car in the driveway. Unfortunately, it wasn't.

CHAPTER 15

Drape arrived at Nita's house later that afternoon after making a brief stop to meet Burns and Lewis for the twenty grand of marked money and the wire. Like clockwork, the Feds were staked out down the street from Nita's crib ready to hark on the transaction. Agent Lewis had another unit of agents staked out across the street from Shorty's hair salon with enough equipment to hear a mouse fart. Unbeknownst to Shorty, Drape had decided to frame her in exchange for Angel's freedom. Drape strolled into Nita's house wearing the weight of the world on his shoulders, and carrying a bag that contained the money.

When he burst into the back bedroom, everyone seemed startled. Tim was smoking a blunt with his legs propped up on a cushion while Romeo sat in the corner counting money. The room had a cloud of smoke above them all, yet Drape paid it no mind.

"Tim you got dat?" Drape asked referring to Tiger's money. Tiger had called to let Drape know that he'd left his cut.

"Yeah, here it go," Romeo said pointing to the bag on the floor in front of him.

"So, Romeo, you straight? Yours there too?" Drape asked.

"I'm in, Drape," he replied.

"Good." After getting everybody to confirm they had

their cut with them on wire, he told Tim to call Shorty.

"What's da business?" she answered.

Tim held his hand over the bottom of the phone and whispered to Drape with a smirk, "Yo', you done rubbed off on her cause she startin' to sound just like you," he said. "Dis Tim. Where you want me to meet you at?"

"Come up to my shop. What time you go to sleep last night?" Shorty asked in code slang. The real meaning was, *how many bricks you want*?

"Shit, around five," he retorted letting her know he wanted five bricks.

"I'm here waitin' so don't take all damn day! I've got some houses to show to a new client. Don't forget I'm a part time real estate agent too, nigga."

Everybody stared down Tim's throat as he let her know he was on his way. Even Agent Lewis and Detective Burns listened closely through the wire Drape had on. After Tim got off the phone, Drape stuffed the eighty grand he collected from his boys into the large duffle bag along with the twenty grand of marked money then tossed the duffle bag to Tim.

"Don't take all fuckin' day," Romeo griped as Tim walked out of the door. I gotta date tonight."

Tim shook his head at Romeo's addiction and rushed out the door. It only took fifteen minutes on the short drive to Shorty's shop and a small amount of time for Tim to plant the seed that maybe it was time to do his own thing; breaking away from Drape. He pulled up to Shorty's salon and parked behind her car out front. Little did he know the Feds could see him perfectly from the cable company van parked across the street. Tim hopped out with the duffle bag thrown over his left shoulder, and strutted into the salon. His $30,000 dollar watch glistened from the sunlight as the Feds snapped pictures like the paparazzi.

"Lock that door," Shorty said to Tim as he shut the

door behind him.

Porsha sat sluggishly in Shorty's chair as they enjoyed the blunt they were passing back and forth.

"Where da fuck you think you goin?" Tim asked Porsha zooming in on the form fitting shirt that she'd decided to wear as a dress.

'Huh," Porsha stuttered with a stupid look on her face.

"Oh boy, you tripping already," Shorty intervened before Porsha could reply.

"We goin' to the cabaret at the Cotton Club," Porsha said as Tim stared angrily.

"You ain't tell me shit about dat." His eyes scolded Porsha.

"Why? So you would have told me I couldn't go out. Shit, last time I checked, you said, that your ass wanted an open relationship. So, I'm open."

The girls laughed as Posha stood up to fix her dress and slapped some oil across her nearly bald head. "You can go with us if you want to."

"Naw, I'm cool, do yo' thang. Whassup Shorty?" Tim asked brushing the conversation off.

Shorty reached in her $8,000 Hermés Birkin bag and pulled out the five bricks. She then sat them on her booth counter. In return, Tim handed her the large gym bag. She looked inside for a hot second before transferring the money into her bag.

"Nigga, I don't got time to count it. It all betta be here!" she joked.

"Aw… dat's cold blooded," Tim shot back.

Porsha's eyes opened wide when she caught a glimpse of all the cash. "Give me some money, Tim…since you doing it like that," she said.

"You got balls," Tim replied angrily as Shorty ignored them both and continued to stuff the five bricks into the gym bag. Not waiting for a reply, he said goodbye to Shorty and then walked out the door.

SNITCH

By the time Tim waltzed back through Nita's door, he was rushed by Romeo who'd been complaining ever since he left and waited impatiently for him to arrive.

"Damn dawg! It took yo' ass fo' eva!," Romeo complained as he followed Tim into the dining room. The rest of the guys followed just as anxious.

As soon as Tim sat the gym bag on the dining room table, Drape began to unzip the bag. "Dat look like some good shit," he muttered as Agent Lewis and Detective Burns listened. It was confirmation that the pick up was successful.

"I hope dis shit good. Looks don't mean shit," Romeo mouthed off.

"I gotta go," Drape stated as he placed the brick he purchased with the twenty grand of marked money inside a plastic bag. "Put dat up fo' Tiger," he said to Tim as he hurried out of the front door.

Drape's conscience ate him alive as he drove to meet Agent Lewis. Never in his wildest dreams did he ever think he'd turn on his friends. It was the ultimate betrayal and something that made him sick every time he thought about it.

As soon as Drape pulled into the parking lot, Agent Lewis and Detective Burns were already waiting.

"Good job," Lewis complimented with a huge smile once Drape got out his car.

Drape looked down at his high-water pants then over to Burns who sat nonchalantly in deep thought. "Yeah, I guess," Drape replied dryly. "Here." He tossed the plastic bag into Agent Lewis' lap through the window.

Lewis flashed a grin as he peeked at the brick and the

wire inside the bag. "Your brother's slate is clean," he said with a wink.

"I'll hit y'all up," Drape replied, before pulling off.

Needing someone to talk to, he grabbed his cell phone off the seat and dialed Diona's number. It went straight to voicemail…again.

SNITCH

Later that night, the scene at the cabaret was off the hook. The parking lot was full of foreign cars and trucks on rims. The music inside of the cabaret pounded so hard, Shorty and Porsha could feel the vibrations as they pulled into the parking lot. Like two divas, she and Porsha sashayed into the cabaret ready to do what they did best, *get attention*. As soon as they walked in, they rushed the bar ready to order drinks. Just as Shorty opened her purse to get her wallet, a big burly man stepped up from behind them and placed his hands on the back of their bar stools.

"Hey G-Dolla," the bartender said as she waited for Shorty to retrieve her money.

"Hey Ms. Mary, Don't worry about it, put it on my tab," G-Dolla said giving Shorty the once over.

"Thank you," Shorty and Porsha said simultaneously.

Shorty extended her hand out for a handshake, "My name is Simone and this my girl Porsha."

Both girls checked him out from the Gucci loafers on his feet to his button up shirt accessorized with diamond cuff links. The brotha looked like he took real good care of himself and knew how to present himself to the ladies too.

"I'm G-Dolla," he replied.

Shorty pressed her glossy lips together sassily, "Yeah, I heard. What did yo' mamma name you though?"

He chuckled, "Gary."

Shorty nodded her head. "That's more like it."

"I ain't neva seen y'all around here before. What brings y'all to my neck of da woods?" he asked filling them out.

"Yo' neck of the woods, huh? You mean my girl Tonya's neck of the woods. This is her party right?" Shorty asked.

Shorty and G-Dolla were flirting back and forth so strong they totally forgot about Porsha sitting there as they conversed.

"What kind of work you do?" he asked.

"I do hair and dabble in a little real estate," she responded then reached in her purse to hand him a business card.

"What about yourself?" she asked.

"A lot of real estate," G-Dolla responded.

"Oh," Shorty said with surprise in her voice. She smiled because she figured he sold dope, but was surprised to hear his response was real estate.

"Can I keep this?" he asked holding up the business card.

"You do that, but don't keep it if you're not gonna call," she flirted.

G-Dolla gave her his cell phone number and let the bartender know whatever they ordered was to be put on his tab before walking off.

"Damn bitch, you lookin' at dat nigga all goo-goo eyed. He was fine though," Porsha teased. "Let's go dance."

The girls hit the floor for nearly an hour, dancing hard and flirting with every baller who came their way. Soon, the cabaret was over and the girls sat in the car of the parking lot rolling a blunt. Moments later, a silver Jaguar slowly pulled beside them and stopped. Shorty and Porsha glanced at each other curiously.

"Who the fuck is dat?" Porsha blurted. The Jaguar's dark tinted window suddenly eased down.

"Damn baby, what did I do?" G-Dolla asked responding to Shorty's facial expression.

"Whew!" Shorty said placing her hand on her chest. "Boy don't scare me like that. It's crazy people out here in these streets."

"I would never let anybody do anything to you as long as I'm around. You too beautiful."

"Damn, you macking hard," she teased. "Good game…wrong bitch."

G Dollar smiled. "Don't forget to call me," he reminded.

"Why I gotta call you first? You got my number too," Shorty replied in a sassy tone.

"You know what? Just fo' saying that, I'ma make sho' I call you first," he insisted.

"Do that," she said driving off.

After smoking two blunts and laughing about any and everything, Shorty pulled in front of Porsha's driveway to drop her off after their long night. Tim's car was parked inside the garage so Porsha wouldn't know he was there when she arrived. Any other time, he would still be out in the streets doing what he did best…cheat. Tim hated when Porsha went out with her friends, especially Shorty. Shorty was a get money chick, so he knew she'd come home on some brand new shit.

"Bye bitch!" Porsha said to Shorty as she got out of the car. After staggering toward her front door, she attempted to put her key in the lock as Tim yanked the door open.

"Bitch get in here!" he grumbled through clenched teeth then snatched Porsha inside while peering at Shorty's car through the corner of his eyes.

After seeing Porsha go inside, Shorty backed out of the

driveway. She was headed to 1425…the place where Drape stashed his money.

"What you trippin' fo'? You knew I was goin," Porsha alleged.

"Who da fuck you think you is comin' in dis mutha-fucka at four in da mornin'?" Tim badgered.

Tim didn't trust her as far as he could spit. Not because she was known for being a hoe, but because it was his own insecurity. He snatched her purse and opened it then dumped its contents on the floor.

"Boy you trippin'!" she mumbled as she watched him ramble through the items on the floor.

"Naw bitch you trippin'!" Tim never took his eyes off of the papers he dumped out of her purse, determined to find what he was looking for.

Knowing she had to get Tim off her back, Porsha staggered back toward their bedroom coming out of her clothes along the way. Tim loved make-up sex and she knew it. Even though Tim continued to fuss, he quickly followed behind her like a little puppy. By the time Porsha reached the bedroom she was completely naked. After she plopped face first on the bed, Tim walked up behind her. He slowly slid his finger inside her pussy and began to rotate it against her clitoris. Porsha moaned as she got aroused from the sensation his finger gave her.

"Fuck me!" she moaned as she positioned her ass in the doggy style position.

Removing his finger, Tim seductively licked her cave as she looked at him over her shoulder. Moments later, he lowered his boxers, eased his hard dick inside her then gave Porsha forty minutes of the best fuck session they'd ever had.

CHAPTER 16

Drape woke up fully aroused. He'd been trying to call Diona all night and through early morning, but she still wouldn't answer the phone. Quickly, he threw on an Alex English Denver Nuggets jersey, matching fitted cap and left the house full of emotion. Enough was enough. He couldn't sit at home waiting for Diona anymore. He needed to be in the streets. Drape knew that sooner or later, he would have to go look for her. So many thoughts saturated his mind of the potential possibilities. He didn't want to think she was with another man.

As he pulled out the driveway, Drape's phone began to ring, interrupting his thoughts. "What's da business?" he answered.

"How you doing?" Agent Lewis uttered.

"I'm cool," Drape replied in a dry tone.

"I was wondering what was going on with you since I haven't heard from you."

"Damn, we fuckin' now? We just talked last night."

Lewis cleared his throat. "We're going to need you to put some work in tonight. We need a control buy from one of the Scrilla Boys." He was determined to let Drape know who was in charge and who he was working for. "Meet me at the same place in thirty minutes."

"Yeah a'ight," Drape sighed.

Drape thought hard as he drove. He hated doing what

he was doing but felt he had no choice. He decided to call Tim and let him know he was already out of the dope and needed nine ounces for one of his little niggas. Tim instructed him to swing by, stating he would be over Nita's house waiting. The snitching thing had become a full time job.

Drape turned into the Wal-Mart parking lot and pulled beside Agent Lewis and got out. His shoulders dropped as he walked with attitude pulling down on his hat. He never noticed Tiger's Yukon Denali in the back of the parking lot. Tiger sat there waiting on his girl of the week to come out of the Wal-Mart. He reached for his door handle to get out, ready to call out to Drape.

However, he suddenly came to a halt when he noticed the hillbilly looking white man approach Drape and hand him a knot of money and a small black box.

"What da fuck?" Tiger mumbled to himself as he examined the situation. He hoped it wasn't what he thought. He watched intensively as Drape and Agent Lewis discussed something in detail. Instantly, Tiger became confused. He needed to talk to Drape, but didn't want to call him from his cell after seeing him with the strange white man. He needed a few minutes to sort everything out in his mind.

After getting his next assignment, Drape got back into his car and pulled off with Agent Lewis in tow. Drape thought he was the slickest muthafucka' alive. He told Agent Lewis that Tim was going to charge him seven grand for the nine ounces of crack, which couldn't be further from the truth. Tim was actually only charging him five grand, which instantly made him a two grand profit. Drape reached into his pocket and counted off the money silently so that Agent Lewis wouldn't hear him over the wire. Once he stashed the two grand into his armrest, Drape displayed a sinister grin thinking he had one up on everybody.

When Drape turned onto Nita's street, Agent Lewis

drove to a new discreet location and parked. Tim was already waiting on the steps when Drape arrived. He approached the car window with the package in his hand.

"C'mon dawg, you betta than dat. Get in," Drape said after he complained about his out in the open approach.

He needed Tim inside the car to make sure every detail of their conversation could be heard on the wire. When Tim sat in the passenger seat, he tossed Drape the nine ounces of crack.

"Is all da grams here?" Drape asked just to get his reply.

"Naw all da grams ain't there," Tim joked.

Drape handed him the five grand of marked money as he peered in his rearview.

"Nigga you paranoid?" Tim questioned.

"Naw. I just want to get from in front of here. You burnt dis spot out," he mumbled as Tim opened the door to get out.

"I'll see you tonight at da club."

"A'ight," Drape responded, before pulling off. He wanted to pat himself on the back as he took another glance at the two grand in his armrest. "Stupid muthufuckas."

After leaving Tim, Drape proceeded back to the Wal-Mart parking lot to meet Agent Lewis once again. When Lewis arrived with his usual devilish grin on his face, Drape rolled down his window as the agent pulled up beside him.

"One down, three to go!" Agent Lewis exclaimed.

Tim was the first hand to hand buy he'd made from a member of the Scrilla Boys, but obviously the Feds still wanted more. Drape tossed the dope and the wire to him and shouted, "Call me!" as he pulled off.

"Damn, I can't believe I just did that shit to my boy," Drape said to himself. He felt fucked up and knew this was going against the code of the streets. His conscience continued to eat at him even though he tried to ignore it. Suddenly, he banged his fist against the steering wheel. "Where da fuck is Diona?"

CHAPTER 17

Drape pulled up to the "Moda" night club and got out his car in the valet zone. He peeled a tip off his huge bankroll and shoved it into the hands of a scrawny valet guy. Girls standing in line eyeballed Drape from head to toe. Some gave seductive stares while others went a step further; licking their lips and sticking their asses out for show. Drape's pinky ring glimmered and caught major stares as he walked toward the entrance of the club.

"O-kay…Yeah!" Lil' John and the Eastside Boyz shouted into the microphones crunkly from the stage.

The Scrilla Boys were doing their usual in the V.I.P. with the countless bottles of Cristal scattered across the tables. Romeo danced around, flirting with all the ladies that passed by while Tim stared at the crowd of people through his Cartier sunglasses. Normally when he did that it was a sign that he was embracing his liquored high.

Tiger sat back in the cut showing that something was eating at him. He was determined to get to the bottom of the situation with Drape. Leaning back, he slouched in deep thought while the rest of the Scrilla Boys mingled.

Drape bombarded his way through the wild and jam packed dance floor and up to V.I.P. "What's up dawg?"

"My nigga!" Tim shouted as the bouncer unlocked and opened the velvet rope.

The Scrilla Boys crowded him excitedly. "Man, we

doin' it big tonight," Tim sang. "Everything's on Romeo." He slapped Romeo's hand while Drape shot him a disapproving look.

Tim leaned in close to Drape chanting, "It's some hoes in dis house tonight!" Drape shook his head. He knew his boy was half drunk. "Yo' you a'aight?" Tim asked with concern.

"I'm good," Drape said in a low tone.

"Good. "'Cause I gotta holla at you about sumthin my nigga!"

"What's good?" Drape asked.

"Porsha think she may be pregnant. She don't know for sure, but if she is, I want you to be the Godfather," Tim replied."You always been there fo' me."

"What? Nigga, I would be honored," Drape responded pretending that everything was normal. "You my nigga!" he boasted then paused. "Man, listen I'm all fucked up. Diona hasn't been home in three days," Drape remarked.

Tim displayed a confused expression. "Where da fuck would she be? Maybe she mad about some shit. Y'all argue or somethin'?"

"Nah, that's why I'm gettin' concerned. She did pack a bag though," Drape added.

"Well, lemme know how you wanna handle shit if you don't hear from her," Tim responded sincerely.

All of a sudden the mood changed. Tim and Drape noticed some off brand Jamaican dude in general population walking past V.I.P with a scowl. He gave them the evil eye then kept moving. At the same time Drape noticed Tiger sitting in the booth with another nasty glare as he leaned in close to hear what Tim had to say about the Jamaican. Drape didn't like the mean mug he saw on Tiger's face as they caught eyes. Like a man, he strutted over to Tiger instantly.

"Damn fat boy! What's dat all about?" Drape asked

him.

"Huh! Right now ain't da time or place playa," Tiger replied as he grabbed his hat off the table. He stood up bumping Drape slightly as he bypassed him on his way out the club.

"Whassup wit dat nigga?" Romeo asked Drape after noticing the negative chemistry between him and Tiger.

Drape shrugged his shoulder, "Yo' guess is good as mine." His eyes glared off to the side. "But I think we might have a problem wit' dat Jamaican Dee bullshit."

CHAPTER 18

After a long night of smoking and drinking, Romeo was awakened from the constant ringing of the phone. He thought about not answering as he lay sluggishly on his mattress in his Bingham loft apartment in the Westbank of the flats. From the way Romeo's head pounded and thumped he knew that he'd partied a little too hard. Not to mention he was still dressed in his Dolce & Gabanna shirt and jeans. He couldn't remember how he ended up in his bed or why there were no sheets on the bed. When the phone started ringing again, he finally answered with attitude.

"Whassup?" his voice bellowed groggily.

"Nigga, we might have problems on our hand," Tiger sounded off.

"Mannnnnn, fuck Jamaican Dee," Romeo barked. "That nigga Drape already preached to me about that shit last night."

"Not dat." Tiger sounded distraught.

"Then what kinda problems you talkin' 'bout?"

A large huff bellowed through the phone. "I think this nigga, Drape is snitchin'. I saw him talking to this white man in the Wal-Mart parking lot yesterday."

"Get da fuck outta here!" Romeo said instantly lifting himself off the bed. "Yo, nigga you don't know fo' sure!" he said worriedly. "Just hold off from sayin' anything to anybody else cuz I know him betta' than that." Romeo paused.

"Maybe the white dude was a fien or sumthin?"

"Nah, that man was too narcish," Tiger said with anger in his voice. "He looked too much like an alphabet boy, nothing else but a FED." His tone deepened. "Look, nigga, I know what I saw, that nigga is snitchin' fa real."

"Look Tiger, tell dat nigga Drape to meet you at yo' house so y'all can talk. We like brothers. Drape wouldn't do no shit like dat," Romeo encouraged. He stood up, pacing back and forth.

"Ok, I'll get up wit' him, but if there's any indication dat dis nigga is snitchin' fuck dat brother bullshit! He's dead!" Tiger exclaimed, while throwing an object across the room. "You know the code of honor."

"Mannnnnn, we'll figure it all out," Romeo said shaking his head. "I gotta get some sleep so I can think clearly."

"Bet. I'll get at you later." Tiger disconnected his call with Romeo and called Drape immediately.

Drape answered on the first ring as soon as Tiger's number popped up on his phone. He was interested in knowing what Tiger's beef was.

"What's da business?" Drape answered.

"Stop at my house around one o'clock. I need to talk to you about sumthin'." Tiger," spat without any small talk.

"Damn, is everything cool wit' you?"

"Yeah, I just want to holla at you for a minute," Tiger replied dryly.

"A'ight, I'll be there."

Drape had an eerie feeling about Tiger, especially with his tone of voice. He knew something was up with him but agreed to meet him anyway.

SNITCH

Only forty-five minutes had passed before Drape arrived at Tiger's house… strapped of course. He'd noticed someone following him an hour earlier and still wasn't sure who it was or what it was all about. He had to protect himself. Drape parked on the street, about three blocks from Tiger's place and headed toward the back door.

Tiger lived in a quaint little house that his grandparents had left his mother near Detroit Avenue. His mother was still fighting her addiction to drugs, so she spent her days at Recovery Services on the 29th block of Detroit. Tiger maintained the house for his mother so she wouldn't lose it, but had seriously thought about using some of the money he was making to get a place of his own.

As Drape walked, his sweaty palm clutched the snub nose .357 in his jacket pocket as the clouds above put a gloom over the city and over Drape's mood. Something told him that maybe Tiger had found out about him cooperating with the Feds. He hoped that wasn't the case, but knocked on the door anyway.

"Who is it?" Tiger shouted.

"Drape."

"Come in, nigga!"

Drape let himself in the unlocked back door and walked through the kitchen. He then took a seat in the living room on one of the oversized suede chairs. "Yo Tiger! What's up man?"

"I'm comin'!" Tiger shouted from the back bedroom.

Drape sat uneasily in front of the T.V. and picked up the half a blunt out of the ash tray and blazed it like it belonged to him. Strangely, Scarface was on, Drape's favorite movie. He watched intently for about two minutes realizing Tiger still hadn't come out of the bedroom yet.

Drape's left hand never came out of his pocket. He inhaled the blunt twice with his right hand happy that it was some dro'. The movie was right in the middle of the scene where Tony Montana shot his best friend Manny head on after realizing he'd married his sister. Unfortunately, the weed and the scene intensified Drape's paranoia about Tiger. *Why the fuck has this nigga been actin' so crazy,* he asked himself.

Finally, Tiger emerged from out of his bedroom wearing a dirty white t-shirt that looked as if it were made for a sumu wrestler, a pair of Nike basketball shorts, and some Lebron James tennis shoes. He plopped down on the couch directly across from Drape maintaining his silence, but never taking eyes off him. Little did Drape know, he had his .44 caliber Desert Eagle stashed under the cushion beneath him. For seconds, they both sat glaring into each other's eyes. Their stares said, they were no longer brothers, and their looks proved there was an official beef.

"What was dat shit all about last night?" Drape finally asked eagerly. He hoped to find out what had Tiger on his period. He could see the distrust he had for him in Tiger's eyes.

"Nigga I seen you talkin' to da police in da Wal-mart parkin' lot," Tiger blurted out. "And I seen dat white man hand you some money and dat small black box!"

"Nigga, I don't know what you talkin' bout!" Drape replied with a straight face.

"Oh, you gone sit up here and lie to me?" Tiger flipped into a rage. He leaned forward in his seat as his eyeballs nearly popped from his head. "Mannnnn, I thought we was boys, like brothers!" He banged one fist into the other. "You would do dis shit to us?" Tiger pleaded.

"Man, get da fuck outta here wit' dat dumb shit! I didn't do no shit like dat!"

"Nigga, fuck yo' lying ass! I know you snitchin' so just tell me why. I know you ain't tryna include us in dat bullshit."

Drape's face froze with guilt. He knew he'd been caught with his hand in the cookie jar. Thoughts flashed through his mind of the past; his past with Tiger especially.

They'd done everything together; faught together, lied together, hustled together, and tricked chicks together. But nothing could mend the broken trust.

Drape's hand perspired more as he clutched the gun in his pocket tightly while thinking of a solution. Meanwhile, Tiger mean mugged him as he waited on his reply.

Everything was silent.

Nobody moved.

All of a sudden Tiger decided to prove his point. "Oh, you gon tell me the truth today, nigga!" Tiger made a sudden move for his gun under the microfiber cushion hoping to force Drape into telling the truth.

By the time he grabbed his pistol and turned around, Drape had squeezed the trigger releasing two shots into Tiger's big bulky chest, knocking him back onto the cushion.

While Tony Montana's famous line, "*Say hello to my little friend,*" echoed from behind, Drape's entire childhood memories of Tiger flashed before him. He couldn't believe his eyes. Tiger lay lifeless with his head slumped over and his chunky chin touching his chest. Drape stood in the middle of the floor in shock. He'd killed many times before, but this one act had taken his breath away.

Within seconds, he'd pulled himself together, ran straight to Tiger's stash spot and grabbed the fifty grand inside. Thinking like the old Drape, he quickly ransacked the place and took one last look at his friend. It was hard to believe that he'd just taken out one of the closest people to him. Moments later, Drape's mind began playing tricks on him. He thought he heard sirens as he rushed toward the back door like an Olympic runner. Just like that, he kicked the door back off the hinges to make it look like a home invasion and fled the scene within minutes.

CHAPTER 19

Shorty and G-Dolla met up for dinner at the Blue Pointe Grille on W. 6th Street & Saint Clair in downtown Cleveland. G-Dolla and Shorty both pulled up to the valet in front of the restaurant at the same time.

"Baby you look fine as hell," G-Dolla commented, feeling the bulge rise in his pants as soon as he stepped from the car.

"Thank you, hon!" Shorty replied, wearing a short black BCBG strapless dress.

G-Dolla watched as her long stallion legs strutted in her black Monolo Blahnik pumps with a matching clutch. She looked absolutely flawless.

"You don't look too bad yourself," she joked as she admired G-Dolla in his J. Lindeberg Jeans with the matching belt, polo style shirt and black Prada tennis shoes. Shorty's thong became moist just thinking about his sexy ass.

When they approached the hostess, G-Dolla informed her that he had a reservation for two.

"Follow me," the cute petite hostess said. After directing them to their table, she placed two menus on the table then smiled. "Your waitress will be with you shortly."

"Thank you," G-Dolla responded.

Shorty got comfortable in her seat, setting her clutch near the edge of the table. She wanted to focus all her attention on him. For one, she was pleased at how different he was from Drape. She could finally have someone who was all hers instead of playing the side bitch.

"Gary, I know we've only been out two times, but I think I'm really feeling you."

He smiled. "Oh yeah."

She smiled back.

"It's crazy that this is happening because I was thinking about moving to Atlanta soon, and starting a new life. I'm really growing old of this city and think I could I really do some things down south," she commented. "Especially with my real estate."

"So, you wanna leave me behind? We just got started."

Shorty blushed. "Of course not. You know this relationship thing is sorta new to me. You and I have only been hanging out for about a week now, and talking on the phone 'til the wee hours every night." She grinned widely showing him that she liked all the attention. "But I think I'm falling for you."

"I'm really feelin' you too. I haven't felt this way about a woman in a long time."

Shorty got hot. "Really, or are you just saying that? I know we've been spending a lot of time together but who else you spending your time with?" She leaned over and rubbed G-Dolla on the shoulder.

"Wow, I'm happy to see that you're jealous already." He laughed. "It's cool though 'cause I feel the same way about you. So tell me, any other men in your life that I should know about?"

Before Shorty could respond, her cell phone began to ring. When she looked down at her caller I.D, PRIVATE came across the screen.

"Let me get this, it's probably something wit' my hair salon. I need to go to the bathroom for sec." Shorty excused herself in case it was Drape. She'd robbed him of the money he had under the porch and was ready to help Drape figure out what could've happened to it.

"Okay, do you want me to order you anything, in case the waitress comes?"

"Yeah, get me an apple martini with Ketel One vodka and the stuffed lobster tail." she replied sassily.

"Alright. Got it, sexy."

Shorty made her way to the bathroom with her phone still ringing. She normally didn't answer private calls, but knew that this call must've been urgent.

"Hello," she answered.

"Hey Shorty this is Diona."

Shorty's eyes bulged. "Yeah."

"This conversation will be brief. I know you've been fucking Drape, then smiling up in my face faking, but you know what... I'm not mad at you at all. I actually feel sorry for you. Drape doesn't want you sweetie, because if he did, you would be in my shoes. You're just a grimey bitch that any man you fuck with will always use."

Shorty was furious. "First of all Diona, Drape does love me and always will." She turned to look at her reflection in the mirror. "I'm his first and only love. I *can* and *do* have him whenever I want."

"Shorty, if he loved you so much, he would be with you, not behind closed doors. Girl, don't you realize he's only using you. I 'm not going to waste my time explaining this to you because you ought to know better. But, I will tell you this. I have the upper hand believe that. Bitch, I'm having his son," she said with pride. "You'll be a very bitter bitch fucking around with me and my child. See, this is not even about Drape anymore."

"What is it about Diona? Drape will always cheat on you!" Shorty yelled.

"Really, well that means he's cheating on you too for a

bitch named Stacy. Like I said, you bitches come a dime a dozen. A woman like me is forever. At the end of the day, your ass won't have anything to show for you and Drape's so called relationship. That little trick money Drape gives you isn't shit compared to how I live! You stay on your back, and I'll sleep on mine."

"Whatever Diona!" Shorty shot back. She couldn't believe that for a change Diona's words stung, *bad*.

"You'll see that Drape doesn't want your tired ass! You lucky I'm pregnant or I would've beat that ass a long time ago. You think Drape or any nigga would wife you?"

"Fuck you Diona!" Shorty shouted. She found her neck twisting and eyes bulging in anger. "I never could stand yo' uppity ass. That's why Drape wants a bitch like me and always will."

"Right, I know what type of nigga I deal with, do you? Apparently not. Drape doesn't give a fuck about you, but I don't have to tell you that, you already know. You're just trying to convince yourself how much he loves you. Keep playing your position so that you can keep my money flowing." Diona said.

Shorty burst into laughter pretending Diona's words weren't affecting her.

"Same shit that will make you laugh, will make you cry. You'll see," Diona spat without giving Shorty a chance to respond.

Shorty stood in the middle of the bathroom floor holding the phone. She was flabbergasted by the words Diona has dished. She hated her with a passion and it intensified her drive to prove that uppity bitch wrong. *Who the fuck is Stacy?* she wondered. Maybe Diona was trying to make her jealous, but now she was in Shorty's head. Maybe Diona knew something she didn't.

Shorty regained her composure so that she could finish

her meal with G-Dolla. She left the bathroom pushing Drape and Diona to the back of her mind. She knew she had to do whatever it took to not let the drama ruin her night.

SNITCH

Drape sped down the highway in his Honda paranoid about what had just happened with Tiger. He knew that he had to shoot him first or Tiger would have killed him. *What the fuck did I do*, he kept saying over and over. *I can't believe this shit.* Drape's thoughts were interrupted by his phone ringing. He didn't want to look at the caller I.D, but when he noticed "Wifey" blinking on the screen, he quickly answered.

"Hello!" Drape answered winded.

"Why are you all out of breath?" Diona asked.

"Nuttin', baby where you been? Where are you? I've been worried about you."

"Drape, listen I needed some time to myself. I don't think I want to be with you anymore." She sighed. "I can't do this shit anymore. I don't feel like arguing with you either."

"Diona, please not now. What are you talkin' bout?" he whined. "I haven't done shit. Why are you takin' me through this?"

"Drape, save that shit for someone who believes you…like Shorty!" Drape's heart instantly sank. "Drape, I need space. Once I get my mind together, I'll let you know. I got your calls and messages. Just stop calling, or better yet, call Stacy." Diona didn't even wait for a response. She hung up powering her phone off in case he tried to call back.

Drape tried to call her phone repeatedly for the next fifteen minutes, but she wouldn't answer. As time passed, he became even more frustrated. He felt as if the car was closing in on him. As his mind raced, he could barely breathe. It felt as if he was having an anxiety attack. Everything and everyone around him was crashing down on him like a ton of bricks. "Who da fuck told Diona that bullshit?" he wondered to himself.

CHAPTER 20

Two violent looking men strolled into the Metro Hospital looking for Jamaican Dee. Word on the streets was that his condition was stable and he was able to talk. Tank and Chop were Jamaican Dee's muscle from the Rock Projects. Tank, extremely light with slanted eyes gave off the vibe that he could see straight through you as he walked and surveyed the area.

Chop was no less intimidating with the many tattoos that cascaded all over his midnight black body, including his neck and arms. His nappy afro didn't make his appearance any better. His face conveyed a resemblance to a bull, wide and strong. When the door opened to the hospital room, Jamaican Dee was in bed with his head propped up watching the small thirteen inch television mounted from the ceiling. The mood was errie since no one had ever seen Dee fucked up before. All kinds of different tubes and wires were attached to his body and the monitor beside him. *The First 48* played on the T.V. as Tank approached the bed. He could see that Jamaican Dee had dropped about twenty pounds.

"What's cracking rude boy," Tank said.

Jamaican Dee turned to look at his best worker. He attempted to speak but his throat was dry. "Hand me, me cup of water."

Chop poured some water into the plastic cup. "Here." He handed it to him carefully while Dee snatched it and swallowed the entire cup. Tank was anxious to hear what he had to say and took a seat next to him on the bed while Chop took a seat in the chair in the corner of the small room.

"So, what's the emergency?" Tank asked in a deep voice.

Jamaican Dee coughed, "Da bloodclot Kim set me up," he uttered.

Tank looked confused as he rubbed his bushy head. "You sure? C'mon, that's your baby's momma, I don't think she that hateful."

"Me know for a fact," Dee muttered.

"How you know?" Chop inquired from across the room.

"De detective come by me room earlier… show me de statement Kim wrote. She say she see nut'ting," Dee paused. "Da bloodclot lying!" he said throwing the remote across the room. "Me saw her looking out de window…right at me," Jamaican Dee explained with suspicion.

"Damn. So, what you want us to do?" Tank asked standing to his feet.

Dee returned his question with a long infuriated stare then uttered silently, "Kill de bitch, 'dem muthafuckas damn near killed me. Me gave 'dem a hundred g's and dey still shoot me."

"How many niggas was it? What about your daughter?" Chop inquired, getting into retaliation mode.

"Me tink two, not sure, but leave no witnesses," Jamaican Dee responded.

"We gotcha rude boy!" they both said in unison.

At that moment, a nurse entered the room abruptly carrying a tray with what looked like twenty pills. "I'm sorry gentlemen, but Mr. Hines needs his rest. I'm gonna have to ask you all to leave for the day," she said politely.

"Me expec'ting a visit from me old friend, you bend de

rules this once," he begged with his eyes. "Let me kno' when he get here pretty lady!" Jamaican Dee responded. "It's very important."

"Okay, this once, but they to leave." She pointed toward Chop and Tank. "I'll let you know when your friend arrives," the nurse replied blushing.

SNITCH

CHAPTER 21

Tank drove crazily in the green MVP van as they contemplated how they were going to kill Ecstasy. They didn't want to waste any time. Per their boss's instructions, it had to be done immediately. During the twenty-five minute drive, they put their plan in motion. Chop decided to call Ecstasy and act as if he were checking up on her. Ecstasy was laying on her living room couch when her cell phone rang. She hadn't been going to the strip club every night since Romeo said she was getting twenty thousand from the robbery. Strangely, he hadn't given it to her yet. She ran toward the phone sitting on the table hastily, thinking it was Romeo who'd just left.

"Hello," she answered.

"What's good Kim?" Chop asked.

"Umm…nothing, watching T.V." Instantly she switched to a somber mode, playing depressed.

"You know my nigga wants me to check up on you. You okay ova' there?"

"Yeah, I'm fine." She smacked her lips and rolled her eyes with disgust.

"I'm on my way there. You got some weed?"

She really didn't want Chop stopping by, but couldn't turn down weed and had never turned him down any other time. He always stopped by the club and tipped her just because he knew she needed the extra money. Even though she and Jamaican Dee weren't together, Chop was one of his friends that she didn't mind chilling with.

"Nope, but you can bring me some." Her voice suddenly changed for the better.

"Yeah, I can do that. I should be there in fifteen minutes."

"Do me a favor. Stop by the store and grab a 2-Liter of Pepsi."

"A'ight."

Ecstasy had planned on having Chop out of her house before Romeo returned from Tiger's. He'd told her that Tiger was having some stress issues and wasn't answering his phone. She knew it was just a matter of time before he returned. The last thing she needed was them bumping heads. Romeo had been spending a little more time with her over the past few days, claiming that he was falling for her. She liked his company, but would've loved the twenty grand he'd promised her even more. Romeo said he'd put it away for safe keeping and would bring it over the next day. Ecstasy felt like he was running game, but enjoyed the hourly dick while it lasted. She vowed to get her money. She deserved it.

Thirty minutes had passed and Ecstasy was so into the Jerry Springer show that she didn't hear Chop's mini-van pull into the driveway. He blew his horn twice as he placed the gear in park. Ecstasy jumped off the couch and quickly ran to the door and unlocked it, never looking out to confirm that it was Chop. She assumed it was him as she hurried back to the living room to catch the rest of Jerry's episode where three cousins sat on stage boasting about sleeping with the same woman.

When Chop and Tank entered, Ecstasy was sprawled out on the couch in a form-fitting mini-dress that stopped just below her butt cheeks. She was glued to the television, shouting along with the audience. "Tramp ass bitch!"

Chop stopped in the kitchen, and peeked into the pot

simmering on the stove. He looked for a spoon to stir the contents inside, but didn't see one lying around.

"What the fuck you doing in my pot, boy!" she shouted after hearing the noise in the kitchen. Yet, she never took her eyes off the screen.

"Mmmmmm,that shit smell good," Tank said, taking a look into the pot too. Chop stood next time to him whispering how things would go and finally took the backpack off containing the gun, tape, and other torturing supplies.

"Don't touch my shit!" Ecstasy shouted as soon as a commercial came on. She darted into the kitchen and formed an angry expression when she saw Tank. "Why you didn't tell me you brought his ass with you!" she remarked. She always blamed Tank for her relationship problems with her daughter's father.

"What the fuck you mean by that?" Tank shot back.

"C'mon y'all," Chop intervened before the argument got deeper. He held his arm out stopping Tank who took an aggressive step toward Ecstasy. "Where my niece at?" Chop continued.

"She's over my mother's house," Ecstasy exclaimed in relief.

Chop was happy to hear that because killing his boy's daughter was something he didn't want on his conscience. "Here, roll something up," Chop insisted as he handed her a sack of weed and a Philly blunt.

Ecstasy snatched the 2-Liter of Pepsi out of Tank's hand and placed it in the fridge, rolling her eyes again, but this time toward the back of her head. He and Chop followed her into the living room.

And after smoking two blunts, Ecstasy was stretched across the couch flipping through the channels looking for the next show full of drama. She was horny and ready for them to leave before Romeo got back.

"Well, I guess I'll go get ready for work," she said, hoping they would get the message.

Tank stood up and eased closer to the window. He looked out suspiciously before closing the blinds.

"What the fuck are you doing?" Ecstasy barked. She stood to her feet and placed her hands on her hips.

"Bitch you know what the fuck I'm doing. The question is what the fuck was you doing? You must of thought we wasn't gone find out!" Tank angrily replied as Chop stood up too.

"What are you talking about?" she asked as her voice trembled in fear.

The sound of Chop's twenty-two inch biceps echoed like thunder off her cheek as he smacked her to the floor.

"Why y'all doing this to me?" she whined as she looked up at Chop's two hundred and fifty pounds of muscle that stood over her. She grabbed one of her pigtails nervously.

"Oh hoe you gone play stupid huh? Tank griped as he pinned her down on the floor. Forcefully, he pressed his knees toward the inside of her elbows as he sat on her chest.

"Grab some duct tape out of that bag," he told Chop as he unzipped his pants. "And hand me my nine too."

"Please don't do this!" Ecstasy cried out. She rotated her body frantically trying to escape Tank's hold.

"We know you had something to do with it. So, I'm gonna ask you one more time, who did it? Who the fuck robbed my man!" Chop asked firmly.

"I don't knowwwwwwwww!" she cried out. "C'mon Chop you know I wouldn't do no shit like that. That's my daughter's father," she pleaded between sobs. She wanted him to help her, thinking that Tank wasn't willing to hear her out.

Chop stood over her head with a roll of tape in his hand, shaking his head hopelessly. At that point she knew that if she confessed she was dead immediately.

"Bitch I guess that's your story and you sticking to it!" Chop stated as he taped her mouth shut.

Tank slapped her across her face with his soft dick as he sat on her chest laughing. He then got up so Chop could man-handle her legs with his hand around her ankles, pulling her dress up. Ecstasy squirmed trying to resist as he stripped her.

"Make that hoe stop moving!" Chop said to Tank.

At that moment, Tank cocked his gun then pressed the Ruger .9mm up to her forehead. "Bitch don't move!" He growled angrily. "Rape this bitch!"

Chop was the one person who she never expected to deal with sexually, and never imagined it would be by force. He always pretended to be her friend, but the fact that he now pinned down her hundred and twenty pound frame proved otherwise. Without delay, Chop pushed her legs apart and rammed his rigid dick deep into her vaginal canal. Tears rolled down Ecstasy's cheeks as she winced in pain.

Chop pounded her insides with such a massive force for nearly five minutes as Tank cheered on like a spectator at a football game. It seemed like eternity to Ecstasy as he beat the pussy up, and her cell phone rang constantly in the bathroom. It felt as if her insides were being beat with a baseball bat, but all she could do was pray that Romeo would show up and save her. Soon, Chop busted a nut and rose off of Ecstasy's limp body. Blood and semen trickled down her inner thigh while her stomach cramped from the trauma.

"Flip this bitch over! I want some of that ass!" Tank exclaimed. Chop twisted her legs to flip her over onto her stomach and observed as Tank forced his bare rock solid dick into her anus roughly.

Ecstasy's moans could barely be heard through the duct tape.

"Ahh, bitch! You feel good. Damn, Jamaican Dee should've let me hit this shit a long time ago," Tank panted.

Ecstasy grimaced in pain. He took huge, wild strokes as if he were in a hurry, until he busted a nut. When Tank collapsed on top of Ecstasy, she lay stretched like a zombie, unable to move. Her asshole felt like it was on fire and the smell of the blood and semen all over her flawless living room made her want to vomit.

"Bitch you better not move."

Tank stood up and walked toward her bathroom while Chop made sure not to make eye contact with Ecstasy.

When Tank returned and they both pulled their pants back up and never washed themselves off, she knew it would be the end of her life. Tank held her favorite set of curling irons in his hand, waving them in the air with an evil grin.

"You know where this is going," he voiced as he opened and closed them, approaching her.

Her eyes opened wide in fear. "Okay! Okay!" she mumbled through the duct tape. Tank crouched down and snatched the tape off her mouth.

"You said okay, right? Who did it?" he asked hurriedly.

"Romeo from Detroit Avenue!" she blurted out.

"Who else," he roared.

"Nobody! I swear….nobody."

Chop snatched the cordless phone off the base and threw it, hitting her in the face. Tank squatted down beside her, grabbing her neck tightly.

"Bitch, get Romeo over here right now or your ass will never be able to conceive again." he threatened.

"Romeo is supposed to be here soon," Ecstasy fearfully replied.

"Bitch I should smoke you right now for doing that grimey shit to my nigga!" Tank said as he reached inside his backpack. He cocked his gun and threw Ecstasy a nasty look.

SNITCH

Tank sat on the couch and began to unzip his pants again as he got aroused looking at Ecstasy's voluptuous naked body.

"Bitch get over here and suck this dick!" he demanded as he fondled his dick to get it hard again.

She crawled slowly on her hands and knees over to him, grabbing his dick in her palm. She moved slowly almost like it was her first dick. She then began to jack him off with her mouth like a professional. She wanted to gag with the taste of semen and blood in her saliva. However, she figured the more she pleased them, the longer they would keep her alive. Tank's legs jerked as he ejaculated into her mouth. He then mugged her head away from his dick.

"You nasty bitch!"

"Tie this hoe up," Chop uttered as he peered out the window.

"This trick not going nowhere," Tank articulated being lazy not wanting to tie her up.

Chop sighed as he walked up to her and man-handled her roughly as he duct taped her hands and feet. Ecstasy laid there helplessly with tears once again running down her face. "I gotta go handle something, I'll be right back," he told Tank " You know what to do if that nigga Romeo comes before I get back, right?"

"187," Tank replied.

SNITCH

CHAPTER 22

Headed to Tiger's house, Romeo flew down Detroit Avenue with his windows down letting everyone he passed know what type of music he liked. As *Project Pat* blared through the speakers he thought about calling Ecstasy. He'd left her house nearly two hours ago and promised he'd make his errands quick. Of course he lied; Romeo never told the truth when it came to women.

Truth was; he'd made a stop to meet up with some new chick on the east side of town. She tried to convince him to stay, but the troubles between him and his crew had him a little uneasy. He wanted to know if Tiger and Drape had talked or tried to square things straight. Strangely, he hadn't heard anything from either one. He'd called Tiger several times, but his call was sent straight to voicemail.

Upon pulling up, he became nervous, noticing chaos on the scene. The neighbors seemed to talk amongst themselves as they tried to figure out what happened. Police cars and ambulances saturated the street as homicide detectives and police officers attempted to gather witnesses and conduct their investigation. There was yellow crime scene tape everywhere.

Romeo's intuition told him that either Drape or Tiger was involved. The neighborhood was composed of mostly seniors, staying clear of any trouble in the past. Then he thought about Jamaican Dee and his crew. *Was this retalia-*

tion, he wondered. Romeo sped up the hill panicking until he was finally able to park the BMW away from the confusion. He hopped out and quickly rushed down the hill, pushing his way to the front of the crowd. Everyone had their take on what happened.

"Ump humph upmh, them boys just won't stop selling them drugs," one woman said standing inquisitively behind the yellow tape.

The old lady who lived doors down from Tiger was giving a statement to a homicide detective as Romeo looked on. "I heard the shot," she told the reporter.

"And I seen a white Mercedes speed off," a thin lady whispered to a frail man in his forties who stood next to her.

Goose bumps appeared on Romeo's shoulders. Everything seemed to happen in slow motion. As he overheard three or four different stories all at once, two young looking paramedics wheeled a body out of the house on a stretcher.

"Now somebody's mama gonna have to go to the morgue to identify her son," someone voiced in the crowd.

"Wait! Dat's my brother!" Romeo shouted as he saw the body on the stretcher. Something deep inside told him that it was Tiger.

Romeo ripped through the tape like an angry bull as emotions took over his body. An officer tried to stop him from getting a closer look as he barged his way past two officers who were trying to control the crowd. "That's my brother!" he kept repeating, bringing attention to himself. He was determined to get a look under the sheet covering the body.

"I just know it's him. I just know it."

Soon, no one could hold him back; not even the officer who felt for him as he watched tears well up in Romeo's eyes. Finally, he snatched away from the officer's grasp on his arm, lifting the sheet.

Everything stopped.

The crowd gasped as if they were watching an emotional movie.

Romeo took a deep breath and stepped back in shock as he caught a glimpse of Tiger's lifeless facial expression. Blood soaked through the white sheet where Tiger had been shot, yet his fingers clutched hard, not wanting to let go.

"C'mon son. Everything will be okay," the officer told him. "What is your brother's name?"

Romeo broke loose, clearly upset and not wanting to talk. As the officer's called out to him, he hurried back to his car overwhelmed with hurt. His heart told him that Drape had taken Tiger out. When and how it all went done he wasn't sure, but he needed answers. He sped in a fury back to Ecstasy's house.

Romeo drove crazily as he dialed number after number, at times missing a parked car and once even running a red light avoiding a crash by seconds.

"Yo Tim, where you at? Call me man. It's important."

"He hung up and dialed again. "Yo, man, this is real. No bull shit. Call me."

SNITCH

Tank ran to Ecstasy's window, peeping through her bamboo wooden blinds when he heard the sound of Romeo's truck speeding into the driveway. He held his finger up to his mouth signaling for Ecstasy to remain quiet. Tank then hid behind the door, gun in hand, waiting for Romeo to enter. Soon, Romeo had unlocked the door and darted into the house.

Sweat poured from his face and his eyes had reddened. The fact that someone had killed his boy had set in. "Ecstasy!" Romeo called out in a distraught tone.

VegasClarke

Ecstasy could see Romeo, but he didn't see her sitting in the far right corner of her living room with her knees up to her chest, sobbing. She had a good visual on Tank who held the gun in hand, his eyes daring her to speak.

"Put your fucking hands up!" Tank demanded as he came from behind the door and shoved the cold steel into Romeo's back. He began to push him toward the living room as Romeo remained silent. Romeo instantly assumed that it was a stick-up. In his mind Ecstasy had done to him just as they'd done to Jamaican Dee.

"You connivin' bitch," Romeo began to say until he noticed how disheveled Ecstasy's home looked. Things were thrown about. And he knew Ecstasy didn't live that way.

"Get on yo' knees, bitch ass nigga!" Tank shoved the barrel of his gun deeper into his back.

Romeo dropped to his knees submissively followed by a firm kick in his back, compliments of Tank. Romeo went flopping on his stomach thinking how Karma was a bitch.

"You punk muthufucka!" Tank taunted as he rested his foot on his back and stood over him. At that moment, he noticed from the corner of his eye that someone had pulled into the driveway.

Chop cautiously pulled behind Romeo's car whipping out his .45 automatic from under his seat. He wasn't sure what to expect once he got inside. He got out of his car, holding his gun tightly at his side as he walked through the slightly open door. He clutched his gun tighter as he got closer, but loosened his grip a little as he heard Tank's voice.

"Damn nigga! You scared tha' shit out of me!" Tank yelled.

Chop shocked everyone as he walked into the living room where Ecstasy and Romeo were being held hostage. "You should've locked the damn door," Chop said turning around to turn the dead bolt.

SNITCH

He hastily made his way into the living room and kneeled down in front of Romeo. Suddenly, he pressed his gun against the back of his head.

"Oh God, nooooooo," Ecstasy wailed, then shut her eyes. "Pleaseeeee don't."

"Bitch! Shut the fuck up!" Tank interjected.

"So, this da nigga who shot and robbed my nigga, huh." Chop put more force on the gun.

Romeo's mind raced with crazy thoughts as he gazed up at Chop through his fearful eyes. The thought of Tiger's empty eyes as he lay dead on the stretcher ignited his fear of death. He didn't want to die, especially at such a young age. He even glanced at Ecstasy and realized from the looks of things, she had been through some gruesome torture and probably hadn't set him up.

"I got sixty g's at my spot," he blurted as Chop cocked the hammer back on his .45 .

Chop paused. He froze for seconds then began looking back and forth between Tank and Romeo. Finally, he decided to send Tank to Romeo's spot along with Ecstasy to get the money. He knew it would be frivolous to kill Romeo and Ecstasy before they retrieved the cash. Little did they know, once they got back, he was going to kill them both. Before long, Romeo had given directions to his place and where he had the money stashed.

Before they left, Tank tried to convince his boy to tie Romeo up, but of course he played big, saying no need. Tank knew they had to take both Romeo and Ecstasy serious. He wasn't taking any chances. As Ecstasy drove to Romeo's place in Chop's car, Tank sat in the passenger seat with his gun aimed at her. Tears trickled down her cheek every now and then as she thought about her daughter. She wondered if she would ever see her again. She knew that if she tried something stupid like making a foolish move, or purposely getting them stopped by the police, he would shoot her on the spot. Everyone knew Tank didn't care about having it out with the police.

When they arrived at Romeo's apartment, Tank had Ecstasy crawl across the seat getting out on his side. They got out inconspicuously with the pistol hidden, but wedged into her back.

Inside, Tank realized Romeo wasn't the best decorator. It was decent for a man's taste, but didn't reflect the type of money he assumed Romeo had been making. Everything in his house was black and white, including the appliances. White carpet, white picture frames, and white pillows adorned the room, accessorized with a black Italian leather couch. Oddly, his walls were painted black. Black and white pictures of Muhammad Ali, Sugar Ray Leonard, Mike Tyson, and Floyd Mayweather cascaded the walls. The red boxing gloves in the pictures added color and flare to the room plus showed that Romeo was a major boxing fan.

Tank surveyed the room some more yet gave no space in between him and Ecstasy as he kept his gun stuck in her back.

"Get the money, bitch," he urged, as he pushed her closer toward the bedroom.

Ecstasy began to shed silent tears again as she told Tank it was in the cushion of the mattress. He quickly gave her a nod letting her know that she needed to retrieve the money. She suddenly remembered the .22 Derringer pistol Romeo kept underneath his pillow as she pulled the black and white suede comforter back from the foot of the bed.

She began to unzip the pillow-top mattress at a snail's pace, irritating Tank in the process. The sight of the money inside the cushion of the mattress distracted him. It was clear he was getting what he came for.

"Move bitch! I got this," he yelled as he slipped his

SNITCH

gun into his waist then slid his arm in front of her. He shoved her behind him pushing her closer to the head of the bed. His full attention was on the sixty g's as he began to stuff some of the money into his pockets eagerly.

Ecstasy slowly took two steps backward toward the pillow at the head of the bed and eased her hand underneath. Sweat poured as she prayed to live. She fumbled for the pistol never taking her eyes off of Tank. Tank suddenly turned around after stuffing most of the cash into his pockets and was startled by the pistol staring him in the face.

His face gave off a silent growl as Ecstasy's hand's trembled. He knew he wasn't quick enough to pull the gun out of his waist and get a shot off before she plugged him. His best bet was to try and talk the gun out of her hand or get close enough to wrestle the gun away from her.

"You don't want to do this," he said calmly as he eased toward Ecstasy.

She reared back, gripping the gun tighter. "Don't take another step muthafucka! Fuck you, after what you did to me!" She choked up again as her hands shook uncontrollably.

Unexpectedly, Tank leaped forward attempting to snatch the pistol out of her hand. When the gun sounded, both of their eyes nearly popped from their sockets. Ecstasy had let off a shot. Unfortunately for Tank, it was a bulls eye. While Ecstasy froze in place, he stumbled back in shock from the small bullet that he knew had entered his skull. He reached for his forehead, feeling the pain intensify. Tank glanced at the blood on the tip of his fingers for seconds, then instantly dropped dead on the floor.

Ecstasy was a nervous wreck. It took seconds before she could get her legs to move. Although she thought about saving Romeo, she thought about where she would get money to hide out. Nervously, she began digging into Tank's pockets, trying to retrieve the money he'd stuffed deep inside. Fretfully, she checked the area one last time making sure she'd left nothing in the apartment, and took flight as fast as she could.

CHAPTER 23

Chop grew impatient as he waited for Tank and Ecstasy to return. He paced back and forth, rubbing his head with the tip of the gun wondering what the hell could've been taking them so long. Beads of sweat formed on his forehead with anxiety and frustration as he thought about calling Jamaican Dee to tell him what happened. Then he realized that wouldn't have been a good move. His boss was no-nonsense and would shoot him if he felt like he wasn't on point.

"Nigga, you and that bitch are dead when they get back," Chop taunted Romeo. "You wanna rob muthufuckas, do you?"

Romeo just listened and thought about what would happen to Angel if they knew he had been an accomplice. He figured they didn't know because Chop didn't mention his name. Romeo came to the conclusion that his only chance of living was to bring Angel into the picture.

As Chop ranted and moved back and forth across the floor, Romeo made his move. "What about the otha nigga?" he blurted.

Chop rushed Romeo. He was so close to his face he could've kissed him. "What the fuck did you just say?" He lifted Romeo's chin with his gun.

"You know it w-a-s-n-'t m-e, ri-i-i-i-g-h-t?" he stuttered. "I- I I mean…I wassss there but it was my boy's idea. And he was the one who pulled the trigger."

Chop went postal. "Who the fuck is this nigga and where he at!" He stood and flexed like the incredible hulk.

Romeo sang without any further push. "His name is Angel. Ecstasy is fuckin the nigga," he added.

Chop had the strangest look on his face. "Well, I'm glad you're a little punk-ass snitch!" he roared.

"Where this nigga at?" he demanded to know. Chop pulled out his cell and called Jamacain Dee to let him know the unexpected news. Romeo knew that was a big problem. He listened as Chop asked him a few more questions about Angel as he relayed them to Dee. Things were extra foul when he told them that Angel was Drape's brother and where Drape lived.

When the call ended Romeo felt good and breathed a sigh of relief until Chop said, "When Tank get's back we're going to get Angel over here too. This way both of you bitch niggas can die together."

Chop turned his head slightly when Ecstasy's cell phone rang. He took his eyes off Romeo for two seconds wondering where the phone was. Instantly, Romeo rushed Chop. They fell at first causing the gun fall to the floor. It started with Romeo on top of Chop, then Chop on Romeo. Eventually, the two lay on the floor entangled like a fresh pretzel still fighting for the fire power. They continued to tussle for minutes until Chop clutched his gun once again and Romeo clutched Chop's hands. They managed to stand, stumbling over the coffee table as they both ended up with a grip of the gun. That's when it all happened.

Gun shots erupted and they both hit the floor.

They both let go of the gun as it went off. Frantically, Chop began patting his body for blood. Romeo tried to do the same but with less movement. Soon, Romeo grunted in pain as he lay across the floor gasping for breath. Chop grinned wickedly. He grabbed the murder weapon from the floor, quickly fleeing out the door.

SNITCH

Ecstasy approached her house slowly in Chop's car. As she pulled up, she noticed her front door was half-way open. Her heart raced even more. She continued to pass at a sluggish pace wishing she had a cell phone to call for help. Romeo's car was still in the same spot which caused her to believe he was still inside, dead or alive she wasn't sure.

Question after question she rationalized with herself. Her first thought was to speed off searching for the police, or asking someone else to call 911. Then she froze, she figured they would want to detain her. After all, it was her house. Then they'd want to make the connection to Tank's murder. Ecstasy beat against the dash in confusion.

"It's Romeo or me," she debated with herself. "Maybe I should go get Tim?"

All of a sudden, Ecstasy pressed on the gas, passing the house she'd called home. Although Romeo's life was on the line, her freedom was too. Taking her chances as a fugitive on the run with Romeo's sixty g's seemed to be a far better idea.

CHAPTER 24

Drape's cell phone rang as he sat in his house mulling over what he'd done to Tiger; his boy. His childhood friend. The one who trusted him most. He had the irresistible urge to end everything, packing a bag and disappearing. The ringing finally ended then began again. Sluggishly, Drape looked at the name blinking on the screen. He noticed it was Tim and decided to answer.

"Hello."

"Drape! Somebody killed Tiger," Tim sputtered. His distressed voice cracked.

"C'mon dawg, you got to be bullshittin' me," Drape replied.

"On the real man, somebody kicked his door in and shot him," he sniffled. "Man, I can't believe dis shit!" Tim's voice alternated pitches; from high to low showing that he was tore up about the news.

"Ahhh naw man!" Drape kept repeating.

"Tiger's mother went down to the morgue. The detectives told'er it was a drug related murder."

"Damn!" Drape yelled. "Who you think did it?" Inside, he was thankful he wasn't a suspect.

"I'on know man. Come to his Aunt Cookie's house, we all over here."

"Bet."

"Wait. You talked to Romeo?" Tim asked almost in a

bewildered state.

"Naw, but I can call him and hip him to what's goin' on."

"Do that man. I've been callin' dat nigga…can't get 'em. He need to be here too."

"Done. I'm on my way," Drape responded.

-CLICK-

As Drape got ready to leave, he heard the garage door rise. His mind was playing so many tricks on him, he didn't know what to make of it. His first thought; *payback*. He knew Tim nor Romeo were on to him, but wasn't sure how long that would last. Then his mind switched to the Jamaicans. There was no way they knew where he lived. Nor would they have the guts to come through his garage in broad daylight.

Suddenly, Drape crept into the kitchen, his piece in hand, waiting for someone to come through the door. Suddenly, the door opened. It was Diona.

She jumped frantically, "Drape, why do you have that gun?"

"Why da fuck didn't you say you was comin' home?" Drape demanded.

"Drape, fuck you." She rolled her eyes, laying her purse down on the kitchen counter. "You did me dirty," she replied in a sassy tone.

"What da fuck you mean?" He moved in close. "You carryin' my seed and got the nerve to tell me don't worry about it. "I mean you spendin' nights out now and tellin' me you need some time?"

Diona shot back with a fuming stare. "You're not worried when you fucking those nasty ass bitches are you?

"What are you talking about Diona?" Drape's eyes shifted. "What's this all about?" He reached out, attempting to grab her shoulder lightly. "I just want us to be happy." Diona jerked away from his apologetic embrace. "I mean all this stuff about other women. I only love you." Drape exclaimed.

Diona crossed her arms, twisted her lips and gave Drape a condescending stare. "Did you fuck Stacy?"

"What, what? Where you get dat from?" Drape stammered.

"That crazy bitch sent me a letter and pictures the other day. Then she said you were also fucking Shorty!" Diona yelled, throwing the picture at Drape.

"It's not like that! I knew da bitch, but I never fucked her, I swear!" Drape lied.

"You know what… I don't want to hear it! You have embarrassed the fuck out of me! I may have been able to get over this Stacy tramp, but you fucking Shorty in my face, nigga please!"

"Diona, don't do this, not right now, please not right now! Tiger was just found dead! Please Diona, I need you! We not gone break up over no stupid bitches. You know I'm a street nigga, that ain't no excuse, but please!" Drape pleaded.

"I'm sorry to hear about Tiger, but I've been away thinking about this. Drape, get your sorry ass the fuck out of my house!" she said looking him dead in his eyes.

"Diona, this my house too."

Tears rolled as Diona began breathing heavily. He didn't want anything bad happening to her while she was pregnant. "It's in my name," she growled, holding the bottom of her stomach.

"I pay the mortgage," Drape said softly. He needed everything to work between them. "Diona, I think I should stay, just to protect you. Look, I'll even sleep on the couch…"

"No!" she fired back.

Suddenly, the doorbell rang. Both sets of eyes moved toward the front of the house.

"You expectin' anybody?" he asked.

Diona remained quiet for seconds as she blotted her face with a Kleenex. "It's probably my dad."

Drape headed to the door before letting a fuming Mr. Young inside. Of course as soon as Drape opened the door his drive changed. Mr. Young had always intimidated him but today even more than before. The two men barely spoke as Mr. Young brushed past Drape and hurried into the kitchen only to notice that his daughter had been crying.

"Let's go," he told Diona. His face tightened as he looked around. "You don't have to live unhappily, baby girl."

"I'm not leaving, Daddy. Drape is."

"C'mon Diona. This is bullshit! Drape yelled.

Watch your mouth son," Mr. Young ordered.

Drape grabbed his keys in defeat knowing that as long as Mr. Young was there he wouldn't have a chance on reconciling. "Diona, I'm not packin' a bag for now. I'll buy some shit in the street. Just know that I love you!" Drape sulked leaving out the door.

"Yeah, I know! Your dude already told me," Diona said slickly out of her mouth.

Drape stopped dead in his tracks to turn and look at Diona. He could see the pain in her eyes. He hoped this wasn't the end of them. He pondered what Diona meant when she said, "Your dude already told me." Who was she talking about?

CHAPTER 25

When Drape arrived at Tiger's Aunt Cookie's house, it was like a family reunion. Aunt Cookie was his mother's best friend who'd helped raise Tiger from time to time. All of Tiger's family crowded in the parking lot of the West 7th Projects. Drape got out the car, looking scruffy. He had on a pair of wrinkled jeans, a Sean John t-shirt and in badly need of a shave. He looked like he'd lost his best friend as he approached Tiger's mother with a solemn look, and his arms spread prepared to give condolences.

"Somebody killed my baby!" she cried as she buried her face in Drape's chest with her arms wrapped around him soaking his shirt with tears.

Tim walked up to them and embraced Tiger's mother in a group hug, crying more than she did. After seeing how hurt they were, she immediately toughened up and encouraged them to be strong for her. "We family. Let's all pull together," she told them. Quickly, they distanced themselves from her so they could talk.

"Whoever did dis to Tiger, we gone fuck dem up!" Tim vowed.

"Nigga, I know. We gone find out. I'ma put my ears to the streets," Drape confirmed.

"I done called dis nigga's phone like a hundred times," Tim announced, dialing Romeo's number for the eighth time.

"Who?" Drape asked.

"Romeo!" he replied.

"Damn! We gotta find that nigga so he don't do no stupid shit when he find out about Tiger," Drape responded. Drape was beginning to feel helpless.

"I can already tell you, I'm gonna get my artillery ready," Tim informed.

Drape was trying to play it cool when his phone started ringing again. "What's da business?" he answered.

"What up? You ready for me?" G-Dolla inquired.

"Nah, not yet! I got you though!"

"Ah come on man, don't do me like this, I need my ends for real. You had that shit for a minute. You my nigga, but I need my paper!"

"Trust me I got you. It's a lot of shit goin' on. I'll have it for you in a couple of days."

"Drape, don't be bullshittin', hit me up when you ready," G-Dolla said aggravated.

"A'ight," Drape said hanging up.

G-Dolla was the least of his worries. He hoped that at some point he would be able to leave town a free man without paying G. Dolla even one dollar. He also prayed that Tiger never told anyone what he suspected of him. Drape stood around for the next hour both antsy and paranoid as Tim mapped out a plan to find out what happened with Tiger. Shit was starting to look real bad for the Scrilla Boys, especially Drape.

CHAPTER 26

Porsha was beginning to get worried about Ecstasy. Since her girl hadn't been to work in days, and wasn't answering any calls, Porsha decided to stop by her house unannounced. As she noticed Romeo's car parked in her driveway she shook her head with pity.

"Dis bitch dick whipped," Porsha mumbled to herself as she got out of the car.

She walked toward the front door that was half-way open then knocked twice causing it to open all the way. As soon as she peeked inside, she saw that the house was messy and the coffee table had been broken. She knew Ecstasy never kept her house that way so concern instantly kicked in. Suddenly, everything stopped. Porsha let out a loud scream when she saw Romeo's body stretched out in a puddle of blood and his eyes rolled to the back of his head. Her screams grew louder as she took a step backward onto the porch. A next door neighbor ran to her aid as she screamed to the top of her lungs.

"What's wrong?" he asked.

All Porsha could do was point in the direction of the house as she continued to scream. Knowing something was wrong, when the neighbor took a peep inside the house, his eyes instantly became enlarged.

"Somebody call 911!" he yelled to the crowd of neighbors who had started gather.

Five minutes passed before the police and paramedics were scattered out front. Ecstasy's front yard was filled to capacity with spectators gawking and trying to figure out what happened. The Shaker Heights Police Department called Detective Burns to the crime scene considering he was handling Tiger's case. Instantly, his intuition told him they were both connected in some way. He grilled Porsha slightly on what she knew, which was nothing. He then gave her his card and told her to give him a call if she heard anything.

Two Scrilla Boys in one day, he thought to himself as he watched Porsha walk to her car.

As soon as the door shut, Porsha called Tim. She drove off praying he would answer. After the tenth ring, his voice finally sounded.

"Damn, what?"

"Tim, Romeo's dead!"

"What?" he said softening his voice. He couldn't believe what he was hearing.

"He's dead! I just found his body at Ecstasy's house." Porsha pulled over to the side of the road as she got choked up all over again. Tears flooded her face as she listened to Tim break down all at the same time.

"Hell nah! Dis can't be happenin'. I told him about dat scandalous bitch, Ecstasy. Is she dead too?" As soon as he said that, Drape looked at him curiously.

"She wasn't there. She missing," she replied. "I hope she's not dead!"

"Lemme' hit you back," Tim said as tears trickled down his face.

-CLICK-

"What happened?" Drape asked with concern.

"Romeo's dead y'all. Porsha just found his body ova' dat scandalous bitch, Ecstasy's house. I'ma kill dat hoe!" Tim yelled. "She betta hope da police catch her before I do," he continued.

"I bet dat nigga Jamaican Dee had sumthin' to do wit' it!" Drape announced.

With reddened eyes, Tim asked, "Why you say dat?" Tim got up close in Drape's face. "He robbed Jamaican Dee so they probably got back at him."

As Drape reminded Tim about the Jamaicain who eyed them down at the club Tim beat his fist one into another. He had no idea that Romeo had robbed Dee. Everything seemed to be hitting him all at once. Tim ended with some news to Drape about a potential plan and how everyone needed to watch their backs.

"I guess I'll meet y'all ova' Romeo's mom house," Tim suggested.

"Aiight, I'll see you there." Drape's phone rang as he walked toward his car.

"Hello," he answered.

"I know you heard about Romeo," Shorty grumbled.

"Yeah, him and Tiger."

"What you mean Tiger?"

"Somebody kicked his door in and shot him and I know for sure dat nigga Jamaican Dee killed Romeo."

"Don't tell me Romeo's the one who shot and robbed that nigga. Why didn't you tell me that when I told you about what happen to him?" Shorty asked.

"I didn't know then!"

"Unh, unh!" she mumbled. "Well, listen…your bitch called me yesterday. I just thought you should know."

Look, I'm sorry about that Shorty. I'll make it up to you."

"Whatever. So, how's all this Fed shit goin'?"

"Mannnnn, I'on know. Lemme' hit you back," Drape announced abruptly.

"Okay, be careful Drape."

SNITCH

CHAPTER 27

Three weeks passed by slowly; even slower than Drape drove down Kingsmen with his head tilted to the side. The funeral's of both Tiger and Romeo had gone by and Drape had begun to isolate himself. The funerals were tough to handle considering they were both long time friends of his. It seemed like every one they had ever known attended the services; even Detective Burns and Diona.

He was shocked to see her when she walked in hoping it was the end of his couch hopping. He'd been staying with his mother off and on, a few nights with Angel, and even more in costly hotels. Life had gotten the best of Mr. Lopez making him want to throw in the towel.

Drape had to reflect on his life and what he'd become. He did want a family just as Diona did, but still felt he wasn't ready for marriage. Drape knew she was the right woman…the timing was simply bad. Tons of thoughts danced through his head. The most pressing; he wanted to go home. He needed companionship, someone to hold at night, and someone he could confide in during such a tough time in his life.

Since the funeral Drape hadn't seen or talked to any-one, except Angel and Shorty. He ignored everyone else's calls; especially Tim's who'd made it his lifelong goal to catch the person who killed Tiger and Romeo. That's all he talked about, *how he'd gut the nigga who murdered his family*. Drape was tired of hearing about it. He wanted it all to go away, along with the secret that he would take to his grave.

Drape needed some lovin' so what better place to run than Shorty's. But when he pulled in front of her house he got an unexpected surprise. He noticed the license plates on the silver Jaguar parked in her driveway that read "INVESTOR."

"What da fuck is G-Dolla's car doin' over here?" he asked himself curiously.

He grabbed his cell phone and called Shorty's cell as he drove off angrily. It rang five times before her voice sounded. "You've reached Simone. Sorry I can't answer your call, but leave a message and I will call you back, thank you."

Drape instantly began to feel she was ducking him as he hung up, never leaving a message. "What da fuck, I'm arguin' wit' my bitch ova' dis scandalous hoe!" Drape mumbled to himself.

SNITCH

Agent Lewis sat at his desk with his feet propped on the top of it. He hadn't heard from Drape in two weeks, so he gave him a call.

Drape's phone rang as he got a block away from Shorty's house.

"What's da business?" he answered.

"This is Agent Lewis, I need to see you now!" he demanded.

Drape could sense some bullshit in his voice. "Where you want me to meet you at?" he asked with attitude.

"Same place as usual," Lewis suggested.

Drape thought about what happened the last time he met him there. "I don't think we should meet there. We burnt dat spot out," he told him. "Let's meet at da Starbucks on Lake Avenue."

"Sounds good to me! I'll be there in thirty minutes," Lewis said, rushing off the phone.

Drape made it to the spot within ten minutes flat. He sat impatiently waiting for Lewis to turn the corner still thinking about how he'd fucked his life up. When Lewis arrived in his dark blue Taurus, Drape searched the area before getting out the car. He then placed his cell phone in his back jean pocket as he walked toward the front entrance.

Once inside, Drape stopped and stood by the door as he scoured the room looking for Agent Lewis who was sitting in a booth near the bathroom. He gave Drape a nod as they caught eye contact.

"How you doing?" Lewis asked Drape as he got within hearing distance.

"Not too good."

Drape took a seat.

"You look bad. Here." He slid Drape one of the cups in front of him. "I didn't know if you drink coffee so I got you caramel macchiato."

"Dat's cool."

"Mr. Lopez." As soon as Drape heard him call him Mr. Lopez, he knew it was bad news. He had been calling Drape up until now.

"I called you down here to inform you that there's not too much you can do for us at this point. You've made controlled buys for nine ounces of crack and you had Tim purchase a kilo with twenty grand of marked money. You also let us see Shorty sell him five kilo's from outside her salon. Mr. Lopez, my superiors feel you didn't fulfill your end of the deal."

"So, what da fuck you sayin?" Drape snapped in defeat.

"Calm down!" Agent Lewis said spreading his hands apart. "You didn't make buys from Romeo or Tiger."

"They dead. So dat shit don't make no sense."

"A deal is a deal," he said shrugging it off.

"It ain't my fuckin' fault they got killed befo' I could make it happen!" he replied.

"Look, it's not my call," Lewis informed.

"So what's da deal?" Drape asked in a curious tone.

"A hundred and twenty months and..."

Drape cut him off before he could finish, "A hundred and twenty months, dat's ten years. Mufucka, are you crazy?"

Lewis ignored his comment. "It's self-surrender which means you'lll be able to go home to see your child born and your family will be able to drive you to prison and drop you off to start serving your sentence," Agent Lewis continued.

"I know y'all can do a better deal than dat."

"There's nothing I can do. You have a set sentence. The District Attorney already signed off on your paperwork. You can't get no more time or less. We could've just gave you six substantial assistance points and three for accepting responsibility, which would have dropped you nine levels from your base offense level. You still would have gotten more than ten years."

"Damn!" Drape shouted in disappointment.

"I'm sorry everything is signed off on and the indictment is sealed with you, Shorty and Tim. We're going to pick them up in a couple of days."

"So self-surrender?" Drape inquired as he stood up totally dismayed.

"Your lawyer will let you know. But probably in about forty-five days."

Not saying a formal goodbye, Drape headed for the door.

"Drape," Agent Lewis shouted before he walked out the door. Drape made a sudden stop and looked at him. "Good lookin' dawg!" Agent Lewis uttered with sarcasm exposing his devilish grin then laughing right out the door.

Drape ignored him and walked out. He never noticed that when he sat down to talk with Agent Lewis his phone that he placed in his back pocket, accidentally called Shorty's cell phone. Her number was the last number he dialed. Unfortunately for Drape, her voicemail had captured the entire conversation.

SNITCH

CHAPTER 28

Jamaican Dee's condition was eighty percent better. Of course he'd become excited after being discharged from the hospital. He was functioning normal except for the cane he used to walk. He and Chop drove for hours scouring the streets in the Scrilla Boys' hood searching for Angel who had a double wager on his head. Ironically, Jamaican Dee was hired by an old friend to kill Angel, the same man who'd robbed and attempted to kill him. The fact that Angel was the trigger puller and the main culprit who'd sent him to hospital he had it out for him personally.

Jamaican Dee sat in the back seat of his Tahoe behind the dark tinted windows as Chop drove slowly. He was keeping a low profile and felt the police were watching him because of Tank and Romeo's murders. The fact they all took place around Ecstasy connected him, since he was shot in her yard and bodies began to drop afterwards. He was exactly right, Detective Burns believed all murders stimulated from him being shot. He and Chop decided to call it a night after a couple hours of searching for Angel.

"What kind de' car de' you say de bloodclot drive?" Jamaican Dee asked Chop as they stopped at a light.

"An old school Chevy Chevelle," Chop clarified as he lowered the volume on the Beenie Man song which played through the speakers.

"What color?" Dee asked as he glared across the intersection at the passing cars.

Chop could tell by Dee's scowl that he thought he saw Angel. His voice raised a notch. "Candy apple green! Why…you see the nigga?" His neck twisted from right to left.

"I tink dis him ry'ch here." Dee pointed to a car passing the intersection in front of them.

Chop revved the engine waiting for the light to change. As soon as green appeared he took off following Dee's instructions to tail him from a distance inconspicuously.

"Yeah, that's that nigga!" Chop mumbled as he drove. Instantly, he got hyped.

They trailed Angel all the way home with caution without him noticing them following him. Chop pulled over and parked as soon as Angel pulled into his driveway.

"We should just run up in the house and kill every muthafucka in sight," Chop suggested as they watched him go inside.

Dee picked up his cell phone and began to dial.

"Hello," the man answered who he called.

"Yeah dis me. Me have him in me sight. Him jus walk in de' house wit' him family. Whatcha want me to do?"

"When he comes out that house and gets in his car, follow him a couple blocks down the street, then kill him. Don't involve his children. My beef is with him. Call me when you finish the job."

-CLICK-

"We gone wait 'til he come out," Jamaican Dee said to Chop as he hung up from the caller.

Chop looked confused. "We gettin' him for you or for whoever the fuck was just on that phone? His eyebrows creased with curiosity.

"Both," Dee answered, "Me kill him twice." Dee smiled.

SNITCH

SNITCH

The smell of fried chicken filled Angel's nose as he waltzed inside the house.

"Damn! I'm hungry," he grumbled as he got a whiff of the food.

"It ain't ready yet, you better wait til it's done!" his baby's momma uttered as she slaved over the stove.

"Papi! Papi!" his four year old daughter, Alexis screamed excited to see him as she wrapped her arms around his leg.

"Whassup baby?"

"Uncle Ce'sar called looking for you," she replied.

"What did he say?"

"He told me to tell you to call him back," she said as he held her up to his face, ending with a kiss on the cheek.

He put her back down and told her to get the house phone. He'd been spending a lot of time with his family since Romeo's death. Alexis ran full speed into to the kitchen with the cordless phone in her hand.

"Thanks," he said as she handed it to him. He dialed up Drape.

"What's da business?" Drape answered.

"Whassup nigga?"

"Mannnnnn, shit gettin' crazy out here. I just left the spot where I stashed my cash. And the shit is gone!"

"What the fuck?" Angel always got worked up just as much as his brother did.

"Mannn, I'on know. But I gotta tell you something big when I see you. I think my phone lines might be tapped. That's the only way they would've known that I had money stashed under a porch."

"You wanna meet right now? Angel asked eagerly.

"Nah, nigga. Stay in the house. Besides, I can't talk right now. Just answer yo' phone tomorrow."

"I'ma be waiting on your call."

"A'ight dawg. I love you," Drape said before hanging up.

Angel could tell by the tone of his voice something was wrong and bothering him.

CHAPTER 29

Another miserable day passed for Ecstasy. She found herself smoking blunt after blunt and hiding out from the rest of the world. She had a male cousin who she was very close to and who knew the do's and don'ts of the streets well. He'd told her exactly what to do and not to gossip on the phone. Her mother had taken him in and raised him as her own when his mother died so she trusted him to the upmost. She didn't trust anyone knowing where she was but him and her mother.

Ecstasy kept the $60,000 she got out of Romeo's crib close, so close that she slept with it. It was all she had. She'd gotten Sprint to send her another phone saying that the old one was stolen. But she still screened all calls. Ecstasy noticed that Porsha had been calling all day and decided to call back.

"Hello," Porsha answered.

"What's up girl?"

"Oh my Godddddddddd. Girl, I'm so glad you okay. Where da fuck you been?" she asked excited to hear Ecstasy's voice.

"Out the way. Girl shit crazy for me right now," she said in a sad tone.

Porsha knew that not only was the police looking for Ecstasy but Tim was too. "So, I guess you know about Romeo."

"Yeah…I heard." Ecstasy responded in a nonchalant

tone.

"I mean tell me somethin'. The police lookin' for you ain't they?" Porsha questioned.

"Long story, girl. I just called to let you know I'm okay. I gotta get some sleep. It's after midnight. But take care of yourself and your bad ass daughter."

Porsha snickered. "I luv' you girl, and you be careful. Bye."

Porsha, the gossip queen instantly called Shorty. Shorty was in a horrible mood after listening closely to Drape and Agent Lewis' conversation. She laid in her bed, crying and contemplating Drape's payback as her phone begged to be answered. Trusting Drape and trying to help him set up the Scrilla Boys turned out to be a costly mistake. She thought about all the time she'd invested into him over the years and how she'd allowed herself to get played year after year. She thought about the many Christmas' and New Years spent alone all because he claimed one day it would be the two of them.

Shorty inhaled deeply as she gathered her composure realizing it was too late to cry. She glimpsed at the bag that contained Drape's hundred grand sitting on her dresser. Her first thought was to tell Tim about Drape working for the Feds. Then she realized that wouldn't get her off the hook. It would only get Drape killed, which wasn't a bad idea at the time. That's when it hit her. She had to do something drastic to keep herself out of jail. Meanwhile, her phone rang non-stop in the background. Finally, Shorty jumped up and answered as it continued to ring off the hook.

"Hello," she answered appearing to be agitated.

"Damn bitch! What's wrong wit yo' ass?" Porsha remarked.

"I was sleep," she lied.

"Girl, guess who just called me?"

"Who?"

"Guess?"

"C'mon I ain't got time fo'...," Shorty cut her off before she finished her sentence.

"Ecstasy girl!" Porsha blurted.

"Where the fuck she been hiding? You ask that bitch if she killed Romeo?"

"You know I ain't ask no shit like dat."

Another piece of Shorty's plan popped in her head as they spoke. "Do me a favor, can you get in touch wit' her?"

"Yeah, probably if I leave a message on her voicemail. Why, whassup?"

"Call her and leave my number. Tell her she need to call me, it's important. Porsha please don't tell Tim about this conversation, pleasssssse," Shorty begged. "I know how you run your mouth."

Little did Shorty know that if Tim found out Porsha talked to Ecstasy, he would beat her ass, or worse, kill her dead.

"Girl, I swear on my son! Don't worry. I won't say shit."

"Lemme' call you back. Don't forget to do that for me."

"A'ight."

Shorty hurried off the phone and got back in bed. She knew it would be her and Porsha's last time speaking possibly. By Friday she expected to be hiding out in Atlanta or locked up. She prayed not the later.

An hour passed and Shorty laid in her bed high from the blunt she'd just smoked. Her phone rang with 'PRIVATE' blinking across her caller ID. She hoped it was Ecstasy but under no circumstances would she accept a call from a private number. After six rings, her voicemail picked up. She prayed there would be a message. Shorty sat up straight in the bed, for nearly two minutes waiting for the screen to read one message. A smiled appeared on her face as her cell phone displayed the words. She quickly dialed her access code hoping it was Ecstasy.

"Shorty, dis' Ecstasy. Call me on my cell number, 555-1905." It wasn't her regular cell. It was a pre-paid phone that her cousin had convinced her to get in an effort to keep the heat off of her. "Hit me back," she ended.

A mischievous smirk appeared on Shorty's face as she listened to Ecstasy's message. She immediately called Tim.

"Hello," he answered.

"Tim, I need to tell you something and it can't wait."

"It's cool, what's da problem?"

"Drape's working for the Feds!"

"Hell nah!" he chuckled in disbelief. "You and Drape in dis love hate relationship is crazy!"

"I'm not gonna lie about no shit like that! Since you think a bitch lying, listen to this'," she said as her voicemail began to play back the message Drape accidentally left.

Suddenly, Tim fell silent. He made one raging sound as Drape's words tore through his heart.

When it ended, Shorty began, "I told you I'm not gonna lie about no shit like that," she reinforced.

"Damn! Damn! Damn!" Tim kept repeating, shocked by the words he heard come from Drape's mouth. "I can't believe dat nigga did us like dat," he grumbled. "I mean, dats my boy," he added both softly and angrily.

"*Was* your boy. *Was* my part-time man," Shorty commented with sarcasm. "Hold on, I'm about to call that snitch, so don't say shit, just listen," she said clicking over and calling Drape. "Make sure nobody around you says anything either," she said quickly as the phone rang.

"What's da business?" he answered.

"Shit, whassup wit' you?"

"Yeah! I drove pass yo' crib earlier and seen dat Jaguar in da driveway," he said to see how she would respond.

"Why didn't you call and let me know you were coming. I would've let you meet my new man to be."

"Yo' new man, huh! I did call yo' ass, you ain't answer da phone."

"Oh yeah! I did have my phone off. A bitch gotta get some dick sometimes, that once every six week shit wit yo' ass don't cut it anymore," she said in a sassy tone.

She had to bite her tongue to refrain herself from cussing him out. He was acting as if everything was cool and like he didn't feed her to the Feds. The fact he thought he was playing her for a fool made her angrier.

Drape figured by her willingness to introduce him to G-Dolla, meant she never mentioned his name to him. She never introduced him to niggas she fucked with because of Drape's reputation of being a stick-up kid ran niggas off. All he wanted to do at this point was to get his hundred grand from her before the Feds came to pick her up and she knew that.

"I'm comin' to get dat money tomorrow."

"That's cool," she remarked thinking of the time she had bought herself.

"Make sho' you answer yo' phone."

"I am."

"A'ight."

"I forgot to tell you that I'm gonna be showin' this piece of property on Madison tomorrow, so you're gonna have to meet me over there. It's been on the market for a while so I'm eager to sell it. I'll bring that money wit' me," she uttered as Tim listened intensively to her and Drape's conversation.

"Dat's cool."

"Oh yeah, I almost forgot to tell you that Tonya, who

works at my shop, her dude wanna cop a bitch," she said referring to a brick. "I told him twenty-two g's so I could make a couple g's on the side. So, if you still got that, bring it wit' you."

"I still got dat, but when you plan on gettin' da money from dat nigga?" he asked knowing he needed the money before the Feds came to pick her up.

"I guess I'ma go get his money tomorrow and bring it wit me when I meet you," she replied knowing that he wasn't going to take a chance giving her the brick and waiting a couple of days for the money.

"Dat's cool, what time? Be mo' specific about where cause I'm lost. All you said was Madison."

"You know, the big green house on 89th and Madison. The one wit' the big Realty One sign in the front yard. Be there at 7:30 p.m."

"I know da house you talkin' bout, I'll see you tomorrow!"

"A'ight bye," she uttered before clicking him off the line, with Tim listening quietly.

"Hello, hello," she said after she clicked Drape off the line, hoping Tim was still there.

"Yeah, I'm still here," Tim answered. "I'm confused doe', I thought y'all wasn't fuckin' wit' each other."

Look, I'm sorry Tim. Drape told me to offer you some heavy metal, if you know what I mean, for twenty a key and tell you I was gettin' it from one of my niggas. I just did it. I swear I didn't know the Feds were involved. Me and Drape meetin' tomorrow so that I can give him the hundred grand from the five bricks he bought. That's why I wanted you on the phone just now."

"Oh, I'ma be there when that snitch mufucka come through the door. I'll have the ups on him," Tim said, devising a plan that included major artillery. It seemed crazy but

Tim wasn't one hundred percent sold on taking Drape out. It was known in their crew that snitchs were dealt a fatal hand, but since he'd already lost Romeo and Tiger, he had reservations on losing another brother.

"I got one hundred grand of Drape's money. I'll split it wit' you once Drape is dead," Shorty announced before hanging up.

Tim sat in deep thought with his hands covering his face. *Damn, she really wants him dead. Shorty tough as nails and here I'm on the fence.* He got upset with himself for moments until he vowed to do what needed to be done.

Tim sat staring into the thin air wondering how things would play out. He devised a plan that would put him on top. He still had that stick-up kid mentality, even though the last time they hit a lick was four years ago. He figured he could kill Shorty and Drape, then keep the hundred grand and the key Drape was bringing for Tonya's boyfriend; which Shorty explained to him it was just a worm on the hook she made up for Drape's greed to bring the brick.

SNITCH

CHAPTER 30

The next day rolled around with Shorty dressed and up early wearing her infamous smirk upon her face. She wanted to get an early start on the long day ahead. It would take both brains and guts to pull off what she had planned, but she knew she had both. She grabbed the large bag with her favorite clothes and the black suitcase that contained $126,000 inside. She sighed, shut the door, and walked outside, placing the bags in the trunk of her car. Everything seemed to move in slow motion as she thought about leaving her home for good. She stopped momentarily noticing that the clouds looked a little strange. For her, it was all a sign letting her know how gloomy the day was about to get.

Shorty rushed back upstairs and left a message for Ecstasy to call her. She then called G-Dolla hoping to just hear his voice. He seemed to be the only thing that could make her happy amongst all the confusion with Drape and the Feds. She prayed like hell everything would go in her favor and that they had no evidence against her.

"You have reached 216-555-1255, please leave a message after the beep," the automated message said.

"Hey, baby this is yo' boo. I miss you and I want some more of that dick. I can't wait to see you later," she said in a seductive voice, then hung up.

Her next call was to Ecstasy. Once again, her message came on and Shorty left a message. Within seconds, Ecstasy called back.

"Hello," she answered.

"This Ecstasy, whassup girl?"

"Girl, I'm not trying to be all in yo' business, but we need to talk. Where can me and Porsha meet you at?" she asked throwing Porsha's name in to make things seem cool.

"I don't know about that," Ecstasy replied feeling skeptical of meeting them. "Girl, the police looking for me. They tryna question me, but I'm not ready for that shit."

"Girl, I'm risking even showing you what I want to show you. My girl Porsha really cares about you, that's the only reason I even agreed to show you." Shorty sounded super confident as she spoke. "It might keep you out of jail, but if you don't want to, that's cool with me!"

Ecstasy became mute for a second before saying, "Where you wanna meet at?"

A grin appeared on Shorty's face as she heard her reply. She rattled off Drape's address where he cooked his dope. "At my apartment. I live on Lorain Avenue. The address is 1511. It's the upstairs apartment on the left, use the back stairs."

"I know exactly where you're talking about, what time?"

"Six o'clock. Is that okay wit you?" Shorty asked.

"Yeah that's cool. I'll see you at six," Ecstasy responded before hanging up.

Shorty had just executed another piece of her plan. It was time for her next move. She called the second district and demanded to speak to whoever was in charge of the Scrilla Boys investigation. "I've got important information," she bragged. She remembered Drape telling her one of the detectives he met at his lawyer's office was from the second district.

The detective that answered the phone flagged Detective Burns over to the phone and whispered, "She wants you," as he held his hand over the bottom of the phone.

"Yes, this is Detective Burns, I'm in charge of the Scrilla Boys investigation, how may I assist you?"

"This is Kimberly Jones," Shorty lied pretending to be Ecstasy.

"Ms. Jones, I've been looking for you. I need to ask you some questions about your involvement in the murders of Randall Hudson and Jeff Yates better known as Romeo and-Tank."

"First of all, I didn't kill neither one of them!" Shorty raised her voice as if he offended her.

"For some odd reason I believe that."

"I wanna turn myself in, but it's gotta be you by yourself."

"When and where?" he asked anxiously. Burns rubbed his keloid. It had been irritating him a lot lately.

Shorty fumbled through the list of houses for sale that sat on her counter for the address to the house. "4545 89th and Madison at 7:45 p.m. no later," she replied as she found what she was looking for. All of the different addresses were starting to confuse her.

"I'll be there," he responded before hanging up.

Meanwhile, Shorty was set on framing Drape. She grabbed Drape's clothes out of her closet that he'd left with her the day she bonded him out of jail and stuffed them inside a duffle bag. She then placed the small .32 automatic in her waist line and grabbed the brown envelope off the kitchen counter and left. She chuckled as she thought of how Detective Burns really thought she was Ecstasy as she hopped in the Lexus. She called Drape as she drove.

"Hello," Drape answered groggily.

Shorty hesitated. "I think you need to wake up Drape." Her tone told him something was wrong. "Guess what just happened?"

"What? You realized you fuckin up wit' me?"

"No. Not at all," she snapped. "Tim just called my fucking phone talking about you snitchin' and that you set 'them up!" She lied.

Instantly, Drape became paranoid. "They said that?"

"Yep. They know Drape." Her words seemed to be emotionless. It was clear she wasn't the same Shorty; the Shorty who would've had his back no matter what. In the back of his head he wondered what Shorty had told them about the Feds if anything. He became paranoid. "And what you say?" he grilled.

"I told him that I was wit' a client and I couldn't talk. He's gonna meet me at the house where I told you to meet me at 8:00 p.m."

"Eight o'clock. Why da fuck would you do dat?"

"Drape, them niggas were talking crazy about you saying what they was gonna do to you. So I didn't know what else to do." She stopped and sighed showing her frustration. "Look nigga, shit been shaky with us over the last few weeks, but I love you wit' all my heart and I don't ever wanna see nothing happen to you. But you gotta handle yo' business and take that nigga Tim out or he gone take you out. I told them to be there at 8:00 p.m. so by the time they get there, you will already be waiting on them."

"You might be right," he uttered, feeling sick on the stomach. If his entire crew ended up dead he would have to answer to the police for sure.

"Nigga you give me less credit than I deserve," she boasted making shit sound sweet. "You know I got your back. So be there on time."

Drape let out a sigh as he thought about what she said. He knew that if he killed Tim and let her live and she got picked up by the Feds, she would expose him. Beyond the shadow of a doubt, he knew that if he let her live, it would be a costly mistake. She had to die.

"I could've thought of a betta plan," he boasted.

"I'll see you tonight."

"Bet," I'll be there.

"Stupid ass nigga!" Shorty said to herself as she hung up. As usual, she loved stroking her own ego. She was really working her hand on Drape and thinking how naive he was.

Stupid ass bitch, Drape thought to himself as he got up to put his clothes on so he could start his ripping and running for the day.

He didn't believe in leaving any witnesses. He was going to cover his ass at any cost. He was going to kill Tim as soon as they came through the door. He would then get his $100,000 from Shorty along with the extra $20,000 she was bringing from Tonya's boyfriend then kill her. The U.S District Attorney already signed off on his set sentence of ten years, so the Feds couldn't renege on their deal since everybody on his indictment would be dead except for Malik, Tina, and her cousin.

SNITCH

Shorty pulled up to the Benihana's on Chagrin Blvd in Beachwood shortly after 2:00 p.m. With it's wisecracking and fast-chopping chefs Benihana's was the perfect setting for her lunch date. G-Dolla's silver Jaguar was parked out front in a parking space in front of National City Bank, so Shorty decided to pull into the parking space directly beside his Jaguar. She hopped out, checked her make-up, and smiled as she walked inside.

She walked down the spiral stairs, approaching the front counter, "May I help you?" the small Japanese man who stood behind the counter asked

"A reservation was made for Owens," she said giving

him G-Dolla's last name. Shorty scanned the area behind the hostess station where pictures of celebrities who had eaten at the popular restaurant hung.

Suddenly, the Japanese man grabbed a menu and said, "Right this way Mrs. Owens." She followed the Asian host directly to the table where G-Dolla was waiting. She was loving the fact he called her Mrs. Owens. It had a nice ring to it. Being G-Dolla's wife wouldn't be so bad she thought.

"Whassup baby? You want some of this dick uhh?" G-Dolla whispered as he stood up, opening his arms for a hug.

"Hungry as hell and you know it!" she replied blushing as they hugged.

They both sat back down at the table, waiting for the chef to arrive so that he could cook their meals on the table. The chef named Brick arrived and confirmed everyone's order that the waitress had given him.

"How'd you know what I wanted?" Shorty asked with surprise.

"I know a lot more about you than you think I do." He nibbled on her ear as she slipped her body in between his arms. "Did I order what you liked?"

"Yeah, that's cool," she told him while tuning everyone else at the table out.

"So listen, how about we take this relationship to the next level?" G-Dolla asked, picking Shorty's hand up and kissing the back.

"I was thinking the same thing," she replied. It was crazy how they sat googoo eyed like they'd been in love for months. "I'm feeling the fuck outta you! What about you moving to the ATL with me?"

G-Dolla jerked back a bit. "What? I don't know about that. I got business here, but I'm willin' to come back and forth for you."

Shorty looked a little disappointed at first. But when

she felt G-Dolla's warm lips press up against hers she immediately got excited. "Cool, I haven't decided when yet, but it's gonna be soon," Shorty said looking into G-Dolla's eyes. "Promise me you won't forget about me."

"Never that," he said turning to watch the chef cook from the corner of his eyes. "I think I've found my soul mate."

Shorty laughed heartily. She couldn't believe she'd found a nigga who truly cared for her. They sat and gazed at Brick in amazement, chopping vegetables and meat while doing tricks with the knives as he prepared the meals.

Soon, another obstacle was thrown at Shorty when she received a text message that troubled her. It was from Tim.

Drape might have to die tonight!

VegasClarke

SNITCH

CHAPTER 31

Drape rushed out of the revolving doors of the Embassy Suites glad that he'd gotten a good night's rest. For once he was able to sleep peacefully without the constant nightmares of being locked up without visitors or commissary money. Drape jumped into his Benz then picked up his cell to call Angel.

"What's da business?" Angel answered like his big brother.

"Da business real fucked up," Drape replied.

"Mannnn, you gotta tell me what's going on," he said remembering the sound of Drape's voice when they spoke the night before.

"I gotta tell you somethin'." Drape paused for a long sigh. "Dis between me and you, okay," he said in a serious tone.

"Go head, man. Tell it."

"I been workin' for da Feds for da past two months tryin' to save my ass and yours."

"What do you mean working for the Feds?"

"I know you remember dat nigga Malik. Well, he set me up wit da Feds. Dat state case Shorty bonded me out of, well, da Feds picked dat up two days after I got out. I ain't let nobody know, but dat nigga Malik set me up and I don't have all da facts yet. To make matters worst, the Feds let me know they got a confidential informant to buy some dope from you," he explained.

"Don't tell me that shit," Angel said as he began to panic.

"I told you to stop dat dibbling and dabbling and let me handle dis dope shit. But don't panic, nigga you cool." Drape grinned inward as he made a sharp left turn. He felt good about being able to protect his brother. "You my baby brother, so I handled that. They squashed what they had on you for my cooperation. But I had to give 'em Shorty."

"What you mean give 'em Shorty? That broad don't hustle."

"Huh, now she do."

"This shit is crazy! So, if you did all that, everything should be cool, right?"

"Dawg, dat ain't even half of it. If Tim call you, don't answer."

"Why?" Angel asked.

"I'll tell you later. Just do as I say. I'ma call you when I finish handlin' my business then you can meet me at momma's house, it's real important. So stay in da house and don't go no where."

"A'ight."

Drape hung up and hopped on Highway 90. He thought about the sound of Angel's voice when he realized his big brother had sold out. Although Angel had been down for Drape no matter what, it seemed as though he was losing ground. His thoughts then switched to Shorty. He thought about her plan and how she'd told Tim to come to the same abandoned property. Drape was going to leave three bricks in the house with all their bodies to make it look like a drug deal gone bad. Drape figured he would be there early enough to kill Shorty then wait for Tim to arrive, pop him off, and then drop off all the money he had to his name with Angel for safe keeping. He'd planned on collecting a 100 grand from Shorty, 20 grand from the sale from Tonya's boyfriend, 46 grand from Sheen, 50 grand that he'd taken from Tiger's crib, and the 45 grand that he'd saved; a total of two hundred and sixty one thousand.

He knew the Feds would be all over him, since after tonight they wouldn't have one single person on his indictment alive except him. His deal was already etched in stone. The Feds whole case was about to be sabotaged. He thought more and more as he drove until his cell rang. The moment he realized it was G-Dolla he sent him straight to voicemail. Drape had no intentions on paying G-Dolla the hundred and fifty grand he owed him for the ten bricks. He figured once G-Dolla got word that the Feds had him, he would be paranoid and wouldn't dare ask about the money anymore.

His cell rang again. This time it was his lawyer.

"What's da business?" Drape answered as he drove.

"Drape this is Mr. Goldstein. I just found out some information you ought to know."

"What's dat?"

"Malik Howard was given immunity from prosecution along with his girlfriend and her cousin for their cooperation and statements against you. That fucking Detective Burns got it out for you for some odd reason," Mr. Goldstein informed him.

"Shit, I don't know why either. Misery loves company I guess. Maybe he mad because he has to walk around wit' that ugly ass scar on his face."

"Sounds like a good enough reason to me," Mr. Goldstein chuckled.

"Good lookin'."

"Call me if you need me," Mr. Goldstein insisted before hanging up. Drape couldn't understand why Detective Burns was trying to destroy him.

SNITCH

CHAPTER 32

Ecstasy waited impatiently outside a bar in Bedford Heights for her cousin to arrive, so he could take her to meet Shorty. The sound of his stereo system caught her attention as he pulled up in his silver Jaguar. Swiftly, she grabbed her Louis Vuitton book bag which contained the sixty grand and hurried out to his car.

"Damn, it took your ass forever!" she complained as she sat in his passenger seat.

"I had to take care of some business wit' my nigga," he shot back.

She looked at the dashboard glaring at the clock that read 5:30 p.m. "It's gone take us at least thirty minutes to get there from here."

"Pipe down. We'll be there by six. Where you say you goin' to meet this friend of yours at?"

"On the west side on Lorain Avenue," Ecstasy said as she began to put fire to her blunt. "You got a charger for this phone?" she asked holding her cell up so he could see it.

He frowned. "I only got a charger fo' my phone. The good shit," he bragged. He turned completely to his right and turned his nose up as he spoke. "Look at you blazin' that nasty smellin' shit. I'ma tell you, I'm only allowin' it 'cause you been goin' through a lot lately."

"You don't know what you missing," she said teasing.

"No, for real though…thanks cuz."

"That mop head ass nigga got you stressin'," he uttered referring to Jamaican Dee's dreadlocks. "My momma always said you lay down wit dogs you get up with fleas," he taunted giving her his dead mother's advice.

Ecstasy shook her head. She loved her cousin dearly and loved the fact that he was so protective, but she wasn't in the mood for lectures. "G.Dolla, just drive," she told him with a smirk.

"Since when you start callin' me my street name? That's a first," he joked.

"Damn, I can't believe I forgot my charger!" she whined ignoring him as they hopped on the freeway.

SNITCH

At 5:45 sharp, Shorty pulled her car into the back parking lot of the apartment building down the street from Drape's cook-up spot. Making sure the car was out of sight, she grabbed the duffle bag full of Drape's clothes and the .32 automatic then walked to his building. She was worn down emotionally after spending so much energy on Tim and convincing him not to take Drape out until they met at the house on Madison.

As soon as she entered the apartment she went to work, grabbing the Pine-sol and the ammonia. Shorty wiped down the cabinet handles vigorously that still probably had her fingerprints on them from the day she got rid of Drape's dope and cooking utensils. For several minutes she washed the same items over and over again becoming fixated on making all her prints disappear.

Soon, she was done. It was time to wait. She walked into the living room and turned on the big screen T.V., pressing the power button with her knuckle. Now, it was all on Ecstasy.

𝕾𝕹𝕴𝕿𝕮𝕳

Ecstasy punched Shorty's number into her drained cell phone causing her battery to die as it rang. "Damn," she said in disappointment.

"What happened?" G-Dolla asked.

"My cell phone just went dead."

"Here, use my work one," he said handing her the phone. "It's a burn out."

She began to punch Shorty's number into his phone.

"Damn, look at that," she announced as they approached two mangled cars on the freeway exit as they rode on 480-West.

Ecstasy placed the phone up to her ear as she observed the wreck from the congested line of cars that tried to move around the accident off the exit at turtle's pace. A Ford explorer had hit a Toyota Corolla from the back, causing the Corolla to spin and hit a cement wall.

"Hello," Shorty answered.

"Whassup girl? This Ecstasy."

Shorty didn't know what number she was calling from and Ecstasy didn't bother to block the number since her cousin said it was a burn out. "Heeey girl! Whassup?" Shorty said as if they had been the best of friends their whole lives.

"I should be pulling up in five minutes. Do you think you can drop me off on the Eastside later so my cousin don't gotta wait for me?"

"Sure girl. You don't have to ask me to do shit like that," Shorty tried to play extra cool. All along it bothered her that someone was with her. She hoped like hell she hadn't mentioned her name.

"Alright, here I come, I'm three minutes away."

Ecstasy hung up and sighed. She took the next two minutes as they drove to complain to G-Dolla about her plans for a new life. "You know I'm thinking about getting a regular job and even going back to school," she told him as they pulled up in front of Drape's cook-up spot.

"I feel you And I'll help you if you serious?" he told her.

"Thanks," she said sadly as the car sat idling.

"You okay?" G-Dolla asked, looking out the window from his right to his left.

"Yeah, I'm cool. These some good friends of mine. I'm just thinking about my daughter. I haven't seen her in a while. Make sure you answer your phone when they bring me to the Eastside to drop me off," Ecstasy said as she forced a smile on her worried face. She was already tired of the fugitive life. She just wanted to go home to her daughter.

"Don't worry about that mop head nigga. I'm gone handle that nigga. But you gotta change your friends. I'ma tell you another thing my momma always told me...." he said as Ecstasy chimed in.

"I knowwwwww....Birds of a feather flock together." She smiled. "How come your momma never told you to stop selling drugs." She laughed wildly and opened the passenger door. G-Dolla laughed too. "Thanks for always looking out for me, cuz," Ecstasy added as she got out clutching her book bag.

"Be careful!" he shouted as he pulled off in a hurry.

"Ecstasy noticed Shorty's car wasn't in the front parking lot as she walked up the stairs to the apartment so she knocked softly on the door.

"Who is it?" Shorty shouted over the loud T.V.

"It's me," Ecstasy replied.

"Come in," Shorty said as she raised the volume a notch higher on the sound system. When Ecstasy let herself in, Shorty yelled out again, "I'm back here…in the living room."

"Where's Porsha?" Ecstasy asked as she entered the living room.

"She took my car to the store to get some blunts," Shorty said thinking fast.

"Damn that T.V. loud girl," Ecstasy said as she took a seat next to Shorty on the plush leather couch.

"Yeah girl, a bitch gotta have that surround sound system. That shit makes it sound like you in the movie theater!"

Ecstasy smiled "You ain't never lied."

"You want somethin' to drink?" Shorty noticed the time on the DVD player. 6:12 sharp.

"Yeah, you got Pepsi?"

"That's a must," Shorty retorted as she walked toward the kitchen out of Ecstasy's sight. She hurried into the bedroom, grabbed the .32 automatic out of the duffle bag and a pillow off the bed. The wall in between the bedroom and the living room vibrated from the surround sound system that was up as loud as it could get. She breathed heavily. Although she had heart, she'd never killed anyone. She cocked the .32 automatic and held the pillow in front of it to muffle the gun blast. Seconds later, Shorty walked back into the living room slowly like an uneasy assassin. From where Ecstasy sat she couldn't see what Shorty held behind the pillow pointed at her.

"What the fu..," Ecstasy began to speak as Shorty released two shots into her face, "Pop-pop!"

Anxious to see what was in the inside, Shorty grabbed the book bag that Ecstasy had clutched in her grasp as she fell slumped over to the side. "Damn!" she said in shock as she gazed at the large amount of cash.

Quickly, she lowered the volume on the sound system and rushed over to grab her duffle bag. Within seconds, she removed Drape's clothes and smeared some of Ecstasy's blood on them, stuffing them back into the bag.

Her heart raced as she tried to think of every important aspect of her plan. It was starting to bother her that she'd taken a life, but Drape had to be punished. What better way than to frame him for Ecstasy's murder?

Shorty placed the gun in her waist line and exited the apartment carrying both the book bag she got from Ecstasy and the duffle bag full of Drape's bloody clothes. The moment that she laid back in the butter colored seats of her Lexus, she knew she'd just gone to the point of no return. After wiping her fingerprints clean off the gun, she laid it on the passenger seat and sat both bags on top of it; pulling off slowly.

CHAPTER 33

Shorty drove nervously through the streets, both hands gripping the wheel as beads of sweat formed across her forehead. Ecstasy's dead face flashed in and out of her mind. The ringing of her cell brought her back to reality as she tried to act as if everything was normal.

"What's the business?" she answered, as a driver blew his horn at her swerving vehicle.

"I'm ready. You get dat money from Tonya's boyfriend yet?" Drape appeared to be extra eager to make the sale.

"No, I didn't wanna go pick up that money from him yet. You know I got yo' money on me... didn't trust him like that," she replied.

"You right about dat," he agreed in the best interest of his money.

"He's gonna meet me at the street over from where I told you to meet me at. I'm just gonna drop yo' money off to you then run around the corner to pick his money up first, then bring him the dope. So meet me at the flea market parking lot first."

"Sounds like a winner to me," Drape grumbled thinking of the extra twenty grand he would get from her before he killed her, along with Tim.

When Shorty pulled in front of the house on Madison, she immediately noticed that Tim was parked in the driveway.

He got out and approached her passenger window with a Glock 17 in hand. Shorty's eyes ballooned after noticing the additional gun peeping from Tim's waistline. His cold scowl told her he was ready for war. Quickly, she held her finger up to her mouth letting him know not to say anything.

"Hold on Drape, my other line just beeped," she lied pressing mute as if she was tending to the caller on the other end. "Yeah this is him right there," she said to Tim as he leaned in her window.

"Sweet!" he said rubbing his hands together. "Can't believe dat snitch nigga thought he was gonna get away wit' dat shit."

"Did y'all go in yet?" Shorty questioned.

"Da door got a lock on it. I ain't get da code from you."

"That's right, I almost forgot. The code is 1000. Make sure y'all pull your car in the garage so he don't see it when he pull up."

"Where you goin'?" Tim asked.

"I gotta stop up the street first to meet my auntie, so she can give me this scandalous ass nigga's money we gone split," Shorty lied.

"Hurry up," Tim shot back. What she said was music to his ears.

She un-muted her phone as she pulled off. "Hello, I'm sorry for putting you on hold so long. Anyway, make sure you pull up the street and meet me in the flea market parking lot before you go to the house. How long is it gonna take you to get here?" Shorty asked.

"I should be pullin' up in five minutes," Drape informed.

"A'ight bye!"

Within minutes, Shorty had pulled into the parking lot, and waited for Drape to arrive. She checked her watch. Like clockwork, everything was on schedule. She hoped that Tim who was only two blocks away had everything set and was in position.

When Drape pulled up he couldn't help but notice her Lexus truck sitting in the parking lot with the music blasting. Shorty tried to act normal as she peered in her rearview at him. He parked his Honda Accord in one of the slanted spaces and got out with the same confident swagger she was used to. Shorty pushed the two bags on the floor that was covering the gun on the passenger seat as he approached.

"Damn killa," he joked as he leaned inside her passenger window glancing at the .32 automatic laying on the seat.

"A bitch gotta have some protection riding wit' all this money, right?"

"Yo' ass is crazy," Drape said admiringly. "You a female thug," he joked.

And you're a backstabbing punk, she wanted to say out loud.

Instead, she did what she did best; worked her conniving game. "Here," she reached down and grabbed the larger duffle bag. "Take this money wit' you while I run around the corner to go get that money from Tonya's." She pointed to the gun lying on the seat. "Take that too."

"I got heat," he boasted.

"Well, this is just some extra power. I wanna make sure you're safe." She grinned reminding Drape of the Shorty he used to feign for. He grabbed the duffle bag and the gun, walking toward his car.

"Lemme give you these bricks for Tonya's man."

Shorty blew her horn and stuck head out of the window as Drape pranced like he had all night. "C'mon boy you better hurry up!" she shouted.

Drape sped up the pace a bit. He opened the trunk and placed the duffle bag beside his cash, and then tossed the .32

automatic on top of the duffle bag. He then opened the back door and grabbed the plastic grocery bag that concealed the three keys. He rushed back toward Shorty thinking he was the slickest dude in the streets. He approached her window.

"There you go," he uttered handing off the drugs.

"The code to the lock on the door is 1000. Make sure you leave your car down here and walk to the house so they don't notice yo' car outside when they pull up. I'll be back in five minutes," she said pulling off.

"You shoulda told me that shit first!" Drape called out as Shorty pulled off. He was pissed that he had to go back in the trunk to get his firepower and two bags full of money before walking a few blocks over to the house. *Did dat bitch really think I would leave all that cash in the trunk of my car,* he thought to himself.

CHAPTER 34

Jamaican Dee and Chop waited desperately outside of Angel's house ready to kill him on the spot. The waiting game had become more than a job. Too much time had passed causing them both to become sluggish and less attentive. Dee sat in the backseat of the Tahoe sleeping while Chop was supposedly on duty.

Angel suddenly appeared out of nowhere moving swiftly toward his old school Chevelle checking his surroundings and looking over his shoulder. His hands were stuck deep in his pockets and he walked with swagger as if up to no good.

Chop reacted erratically when he saw Angel strutting. "Oh, shit! There he go! The nigga on the move!"

Dee opened the back car door in an attempt to get out, but Angel had already gotten in, started the engine and pulled off. By the time Chop got the truck in gear, they were four cars back wondering where the fuck he was going. Dee became antsy, jumping around in the back seat while Chop drove like a bat out of hell.

"What the fuck! You bumbaclot wasn't watching!" Dee blasted.

"This is bullshit!" Chop shouted as he banged on the dash. "The nigga came out of nowhere." He was tired of playing cat and mouse games with Angel. If he were calling the shots he would've burst into Angels' house and killed everyone. But Dee and his special friend for some reason didn't want shit done that way.

Chop and Jamaican Dee followed him desperately dipping in and out of traffic attempting to catch up to Angel.

"Faster!" Dee ordered.

"We should've smoked his ass right in his front yard," Chop suggested as Angel gained distance on them unintentionally.

Angel never noticed Jamaican Dee's Tahoe three cars in back of him because his mind was too busy concentrating on Drape as the red light on West Boulevard caught him. Angel sat bobbing his head to Tupac's song *"Hit 'Em Up"* as the Tahoe pulled up beside him gradually. Angel glanced then turned away adjusting the volume on the dial. His fingers played a tune on the wheel as he held his foot slightly above the gas pedal waiting for the light to change.

Suddenly, a horn blew. Angel turned both ways attempting to catch a glimpse of the impatient driver. In a blink of an eye, Jamaican Dee had rolled down the rear window where he sat and clutched the powerful AK-47 machine gun pointed directly at Angels' temple.

Angel's eyes enlarged. As he gasped for breath his foot touched the gas at the same time the gun erupted. The only thing he knew to do was crouch down in the seat as he attempted to speed off quickly.

Blaaaaaaaaaaat!!! Jamaican Dee squeezed the trigger letting off a round into Angel's driver side door and window. The sound roared resembling battle sounds on a battlefield. The first two slugs that pierced the Chevelle door ripped through Angel's chest like a fierce hurricane at landfall. The car zig-zagged out of control until suddenly, a third slug barraged through the window striking him in the head, killing him instantly.

"That's what the fuck I'm talkin' about!" Chop hollered like they'd just won a victory.

Dee remained silent with a smile of triumph while he watched Angel's car ride on auto-pilot ending with a crash into a tall, light pole. As the Tahoe drove by slowly, Angel's chest could be seen laid across the wheel and his face, life-less.

"Bulls eye," Dee uttered, as he rested his head on the back seat. "Pull off!"

SNITCH

Detective Burns and Agent Lewis left the local nar-cotics station with twelve officers as a part of their brigade. They rolled down the highway headed to 89Th and Madison with lights blaring and squad cars sounding like the President was a part of their convoy. Burns had no intention on meeting Ecstasy alone. She was considered armed and dangerous. He and Agent Lewis weren't going to take any chances with her because Romeo's murder was a staggering blow to their case against the Scrilla Boys.

As Lewis and Burns got closer, a word was given to cut the lights and turn off all sirens. As the brigade pulled up the street from the empty house Lewis observed Drape walk-ing down the street.

Burns eyebrows crinkled. "What the fuck is he doing here?" he asked as Lewis was in the middle of dispersing offi-cers all around the house. "This is getting good. That's Ce'sar Lopez aka Drape," he told everyone who was listening.

They noticed that Drape carried two bags as he walked up the driveway headed to the lockbox. Lewis began shaking his head back and forth.

Everything was silent until Burns spoke in amaze-ment. "You think he knows the code?" He paused, grabbing the bottom of his chin. "This is all too weird."

"Assume your positions," Agent Lewis said over the walkie-talkie, letting everyone know to stay unseen. He shook his head once more.

The Feds had no clue Shorty had just pulled off five minutes before they arrived, or that Tim was inside the house. They were just expecting to apprehend Ecstasy at this location, who supposedly called Detective Burns and told him to meet her at the house.

Just as Burns suspected, Drape entered the code then disappeared inside. The house was empty, reeking of a musty smell and felt creepy as Drape looked at the crown molding on custom features of the house. Drape crept along the center of the foyer checking things out, trying to figure out where he would wait for Tim to arrive.

It was dim throughout the house, except for a light bulb, which hung from the ceiling uncovered. It blinked a few times making Drape think it would go out soon. Although he kept his head tilted to the tall cathedral ceiling, his side vision could see the kitchen ahead. That's when he decided the kitchen would be the perfect spot to get the jump on Tim.

Unbeknownst to him the plan would not work. Drape took three more steps and froze. Surprisingly, Tim was in front of him with his gun pointed directly at his head

"Bring yo' rat ass over here," Tim demanded.

"Whoaaaaaa." Drape held his hands in the air as a sign of surrender, then dropped the bags onto the floor. "You need to chill nigga," he told Tim, as his eyes popped to the forefront of his head. "What's dis all about , dawg?"

Tim kept his hand planted firmly around his steel and his face bawled up like an angry pit bull. "Shut da fuck up! You been playin' me from day one. Yous a muthafuckin' SNITCH!" Tim projected his voice then spit off to the side.

"C,mon dawg, put the gun down and let's talk about

dis."

Drape's hands were becoming tired as he continued to hold them in the air. He hated the fact that he couldn't get to his gun stuffed between his waist line in the back of his pants.

"Nah, fuck dat. You know da honor code"

"Tim, dis me, dawg. Yo brutha. Yo life time friend. Where you gettin' dis shit from, man?"

"Nigga, don't try to snake yo' way outta dis shit. Just like you been trickin' Diona all these years."

Drape instantly developed a strange look across his face. "What she got to do wit' this?"

"I put a bug in her ear about yo' rat ass," Tim informed.

"What nigga?" Drape yelled, remembering Diona's comment from the other day.

"You heard me!" Tim hollered back. "Man, Shorty told me what's up. Move away from those bags." He moved his gun back and forth. "You owe me, nigga. Dat money is mine."

Drape reluctantly took two steps away from the bags wondering how Tim knew it was money inside. One bag contained the money Shorty had given him and the other held the money he'd brought with him. He then thought about Shorty. He knew she was a slick bitch, but never thought she'd backstab him. However, the fact that she still wasn't back told him that he'd been played.

Tim jerked forward to grab the bags from the floor as Drape watched with concentration. Everyone knew he was quick on his feet, but when he quickly grabbed his .357 snub nose from his backside it shocked them both.

"Don't move muthafucka!" Drape warned Tim as they stood face to face.

It was like something out of an old western movie where it was certain someone would die. Tim's scowl was more pronounced than Drape's as he told Drape that he defied everything that hustling stood for. He was hurt, damn near wanted to cry, but couldn't because he knew what had to be done.

Meanwhile, Agent Lewis and Detective Burns grew more curious after seeing Drape go into the house. Moments later, they gave orders for the agents and detectives to move in closer.

"Stand by until I say different," Agent Lewis said over the walkie-talkie.

The agents and detectives covered every possible exit of the house yet none were stationed a few yards away to see Shorty pull up in her car for a front row seat.

Drape and Tim went back and forth taunting demands for the other to drop their weapons. The face off seemed to get louder and louder as one of the officers on the side of the house heard the argument and signaled Lewis.

"I said don't move muthafucka!" Drape yelled as Tim flinched. "Give me one reason why I shouldn't blast yo' ass right now!"

Tim made another sudden move and Drape instantly let off a shot, causing Tim to bust off too. Drape dove off to the side while Tim wasn't as flexible with his ducking skills. Both bullets pierced through Tim's chest as he got caught in the crossfire. He fell to the floor, gasping for breath.

When gunshots were heard from outside, Lewis instantly ordered the agents and detectives to move in. The door flew off the hinges and the Feds swarmed inside screaming, "F.B.I." as they came in. Detective Burns headed straight for Drape who was on his knees with his hands in the air. Burns pointed at the back of Drape's head telling him, "This is the end of you, Mr. Lopez."

"Call an ambulance!" Agent Lewis yelled as he crouched down beside Tim who was coughing up blood. "I don't think he's gonna make it!"

Agents swarmed every room in the house finding nothing but Drape, Tim, and the two bags Drape carried inside. Lewis grabbed them both, opening one to find a bunch of clothes, mostly bloody. Drape's heart sank as he realized what Shorty had done. He just didn't know who's blood it was. *Damn*, he thought.

Drape was brought out like a celebrity with an entourage all around him, yet his hands were cuffed behind his back. As they placed him in the back of a squad car, Shorty watched from the comfort of her Lexus with a mischievous grin. *Damn dat bitch got me good*, Drape thought to himself as he sat in the back of the police car.

Shorty picked up her cell phone as she snacked on a bag of Doritos.

"Hello, Officer London speaking. How may I help you?"

"Please connect me to Detective Burns, it's very important concerning a murder," Shorty stated firmly.

She waited for an answer as Detective Burns cell phone began to ring. As he stood beside the police car Drape sat in, he wondered where the hell Ecstasy was. He answered his phone thinking it might've been her.

"Hello," he answered.

"I would like to report a murder," Shorty said.

"Yeah go ahead," he listened with confusion written all over his face.

"Ms. Kimberly Jones is layin' dead as we speak in Ce'sar Lopez's apartment on Lorain Avenue. The address is 1511."

"Kimberly Jones," he said loud enough for Agent Lewis to hear causing him to move in closer.

"Yeah, Kimberly Jones," Shorty replied as she pulled off.

Before he could ask her how she knew, the dial tone echoed in his ear.

"That was Ms. Jones?" Agent Lewis asked him.

"No, that was somebody saying she's lying dead as we speak in his apartment," Burns said pointing at Drape. Drape listened but had no clue who Kimberly Jones was. He knew her by Ecstasy.

"Who was it that called?" Lewis questioned.

"I don't know. They hung up before I could get that information, but it was a female," Burns replied.

Lewis and Burns immediately radioed for a couple of squad cars to check out the tip they just got. Within minutes, Detective Burn's cell phone rang again.

"What you got for me?" he answered thinking it was the call he had been expecting.

"Yeah Burns this is Detective Obowski. I'm here at the apartment on Lorain Avenue. Ms. Jones is here... dead with two bullets in her face. I checked with the landlord and the apartment is leased to Ce'sar Lopez."

"Make sure you get all the evidence you can from the scene. I mean sweep it clean!" Burns bellowed before hanging up. He then turned to Drape with a weird grin. *You know this is a personal victory for me, right?*

CHAPTER 35

Drape's mind raced with thoughts as he sat at a steel table in the small, 12 by 12 interrogation room. A dim light hung over him, as Detective Burns sat at the other end grilling him. Burns spoke like a confused child wanting answers, "So, you killed Ecstasy, then attempted to kill Tim. I wonder are you responsible for the deaths of Romeo and Tiger too?"

Drape remained calm. "I need to talk to my lawyer," he told him without making eye contact. He then played with his fingers interlocking them as Burns continued.

"I can't believe you would kill your own crew? Wow!" he taunted in an exciting tone. "I know you kill other people without a care in the world, but your own friends. No respect for life!" He banged his fist against the table.

Drape wondered if there were any hidden two way mirrors or a way for others to see what was going on. He'd heard about police brutality but had never been a victim. Burns seemed to be going off the deep end and Drape could only hope that another detective was nearby to assist. Drape refused to look at Burns as his tone deepened and appeared sadistic.

"Drape, Drape, Drape. That's a name I could never forget as long as I live." His tone become enraged. "You might as well confess to killing Ms. Jones. Her body was found with your prints all over it, along with her blood all over your

-218-

clothes."

"Why would I confess to somethin' I didn't do?" Drape asked nonchalantly.

"You listen here you piece of shit, I'm going to make sure this one sticks if you did it or not," Detective Burns said pounding his fist on top of the table again.

Burns rose up and walked around to where Drape sat with his eyes focused. He stood behind Drape for several seconds before suddenly grasping the back of Drape's head mashing it down on the table. Drape laid his arm flat across the table as a sign of helplessness. He knew he was about to get abused by the police. Strangely, Burns grabbed Drape's hand and snatched his large diamond pinky ring off.

"I think this belongs to me!" he mumbled as Drape looked at him in confusion. He watched as Burns placed the pinky ring on his finger.

"Man, give me my shit! I need to call my lawyer, now!" Drape demanded.

"A lawyer can't help you," Burns teased.

Drape paused then rambled a few thoughts through his mind. "Look. I got money and somebody I can give you," Drape said desperately.

"I wouldn't give a fuck if you told me where Osama bin Laden was. You're fucking lucky you're just going to prison 'cause if it were up to me, you would be dead. I want you to feel what I felt three years ago."

Drape stared at him even more confused than before as he thought about what he had just said. Shorty's whole plan unfolded right before him. She had set him up perfectly. He had placed his fingerprints on the gun when he grabbed it off of her seat. And to add insult injury, Detective Burns had a vendetta against him.

Detective Burns cell phone rang as he sat at the table across from Drape. "Hello, Burns," he answered.

"Yeah, dis me. Me kill de blood clot brotha," Jamaican Dee announced.

A smiled appeared on Detective Burn's face as he stared at Drape with a devilish glare in his eye. "Good job. I should have your money for you in a couple of days. I'll call you," he replied.

Burns reached into his back pocket and pulled out his wallet. Fumbling through it for a second, he finally pulled out a picture then sliding it across the table to Drape who stared at the familiar face as if he had seen a ghost. It was the old timer Roscoe who he had murdered three years ago in front of his younger brother, Marc. He glanced up at Detective Burns instantly having a flashback to the day he and the Scrilla Boys were in Roscoe's house. He reminisced on how Detective Burns got the ugly keloid scar on his face.

"Yeah, I'm the little brother you let live," he told Drape confirming what he was thinking.

"You should've killed me when you had the chance. For the first two years after my brother's death, I tried to put a face with your name. I busted my ass as a patrol officer snatching up petty pushers trying to get close to you until I came across Mr. Howard, who ratted on enough muthafuckas for me to get promoted to detective in the narcotics unit. And now you're going to jail for several murders. I've got all the proof I need, caught at the crime scene by several officers and agents." He laughed again and began pacing around the room. "I'm going to let you in on a little secret, you killed my brother, I got yours killed. Now, we're even," he said laughing.

Drape's face sulked and his heart sank into his stomach as he thought about the possibility of Angel being dead. "Nah, he said shaking his head from right to left. "You wouldn't do dat. You a cop, man. You a cop, he kept repeating."

"First and foremost, I'm a man who misses his brother

because of some punk!" he said leaning close to Drape's grim face. "Now, you go to the morgue and identify your brother the way I had to for mine."

CHAPTER 36

Shorty sat Indian-style at the Hilton counting the $170,000 which covered the king sized bed. The room with its red and gold décor and oversized fluffy pillows seemed to be just what the doctor ordered; safety, and a place to rest her head other than a 4x4 cell. A desk, television, and refrigerator filled the room, but nothing impressed Shorty more than the Jacuzzi which sat outside the shower.

The thought of her and G-Dolla fucking like two love birds caused her to raise up off the bed and throw on some slippers. Quickly, Shorty exited the room, rushing downstairs to a payphone. G-Dolla had been on her heart and in her mind all day. She knew he was the one for her, but her current situation presented a problem. By the time the sun came up the following day she'd planned on leaving for Atlanta, with or without him. She finally had enough money to give her the boost she needed in the real estate game and simply wanted someone who truly cared for her to come along.

Shorty knew the only way they could be together was if he came along. There was no way she could stay in Cleveland with the Feds looking for her. She knew if she stayed it would only be a matter of time before they caught her. Knowing it was only right, she planned on coming clean with G-Dolla about everything she'd gone through.

As Shorty rushed through the lobby she began reciting in her mind what she would say when he answered. She wasn't sure if he'd been looking for her considering that she'd dumped her cell phone into the garbage before checking into the hotel. For her, her past would soon be erased.

"Hello."

"Hello," he answered unsteadily. "Who is this?'

"What's the business?" Shorty asked.

"Shit, just wakin' up."

"You don't sound happy to hear from me," Shorty exclaimed in a happy tone.

"Neva that."Strangely, his voice remained monotone. "What phone you callin' from?" he inquired not noticing the number on his caller I.D.

"Long story," she said avoiding his question.

"I got time," he told her sounding a bit annoyed. "You got game."

"No, I know I was supposed to call you, but I just got in a jam," she explained.

"I'm on my way over there," he insisted. "We need to talk."

"I'm not at home."

"Where you at then?" G- Dolla questioned like a jealous boyfriend. "You wit' a nigga?'"

"I'm at a hotel"

"A hotel! What's that all about?"

Shorty covered the phone slightly as she watched over her shoulder at a scrawny white man who seemed to take more interest in her than he should have. She began to whisper, keeping her good eye on the mysterious guy. "Somebody broke into my house yesterday. I wasn't about to sleep in there wit' the lock broke," she lied.

"Why didn't you just call me? You could've stayed over here. You didn't have to spend money on no damn hotel room," he suggested.

"Shit, it's already done now." She smiled realizing he did care for her. "A bitch would be a lot betta if she had some dick over here," she hinted.

"What hotel you at?" he asked eagerly.

"I'm at the Hilton in Macedonia. Room 304. Hurry up, my pussy wetter than a muthafucka," she said seductively.

"Keep it just like it is, I'm on my way."

"Bye," she said in a muffled sound. She hung up and eyed the stranger still watching her every move. "Can I fuckin' help you?" she boldly asked.

"I hope so," he asked with a grin. "I'd like to get to know you better."

Shorty flipped him off as she strutted swiftly toward the elevators. "Fuck off," she told him. "I'm engaged. My man wouldn't like that," she spat, walking off happy that it was just an admirer.

Shorty rushed back upstairs to freshen up before her date arrived. While in the shower, she decided she would tell him her version of the truth. She let the hot water run all over her body as she envisioned G-Dolla kissing her from head to toe. She gripped her firm breasts, pulling her nipple up to her mouth and sucking on it. She then started fingering herself at such a rapid rate that she had an orgasm right in the shower. *Damn, where you at G-Dolla,* she thought to herself. After finishing her shower, she went into her suitcase and pulled out an extra small t-shirt that made her breast look huge. She squeezed into the skimpy shirt that stopped just above her waist revealing her naked perfectly shaped ass. She impatiently waited for G-Dolla by twisting a blunt, and blazing it. This immediately sent her hormones over the top.

SNITCH

Meanwhile, G-Dolla pushed his Jaguar to the limit eager to get to the hotel. Turn after turn he played in his mind how he'd ask Shorty the question. He'd been thinking about her all day and couldn't wait to be face-to-face. He spotted the Lexus in the parking lot as soon as he pulled up and could only rub his chin in deep thought. *Where had she really been*? he wondered.

Before long, he found himself on the elevator sporting some loose fitting jeans and a white graphic t-shirt, with his pistol stuffed deep in his pants. Of course he swagga walked to room 304 like he was performing for the ladies. Unfortunately, there was no one around, making the floor seem abandoned. But by the time he knocked on the door his confidence had faded a bit, after getting no answer, this time he banged.

"Shorty!" he called out, then checked the hallway to make sure no one was watching.

"Who is it?" she asked as she peered through the peephole at him.

He noticed the darkness fill the peephole, "Stop playin', it's me. Open up, girl."

"Who is you?" she continued to play in a seductive voice.

Finally, the door opened slowly exposing Shorty who stood behind the slightly cracked door hiding the fact she was naked from the waist down. "C'mon in here," she said stepping back from the door and looking him up and down seductively as he stepped inside. She made a 180-turn toward the bed and suddenly stopped as she admired her figure in the mirror on the wall.

"Yeah, you made my ass fat like this," she teased as she tried to look at her ass from over her shoulder.

G-Dolla stepped up from behind her and wrapped his arms around her waist. They modeled how good they looked together in the mirror.

"Damn we look good," she mumbled.

At that moment, he wrapped tightly around her waist. His dick instantly got aroused as she pressed her soft ass against his hardened piece and gyrated like she'd just been served the best feeling in life. Shorty leaned her head back over her shoulder and let out a moan from the sensation his finger provided. G-Dolla returned the sentiment with a sensual lick across her cheek while fumbling to loosen his belt.

It was clear the two were in heat. Losing control, G-Dollar nudged Shorty slightly, as she fell to the bed submissively from the push he'd given her. Soon, Shorty lay flat on her stomach, moaning repeatedly as he crouched down and aroused her with his superior pussy eating skills from behind. His tongue plunged in and out of her honey filled hole as he talked nasty hoping to make her even hornier

"Oh baby! That shit feels so good!" Shorty panted, feeling dizzy from the sensation.

He then took his tongue and licked the inside of her ass hole.

"Oh, my God!" she squirmed to edge of the bed where he suddenly caught a glimpse at the stack of cash from her duffle bag as he continued to eat her out. G-Dolla raised off his knees just a notch to look at himself in the mirror. He caught a peep of the cash too through the mirror, but never let on that he saw the money.

"How you want this pussy," she moaned, gyrating her ass cheeks up and down.

"Just like this." He propped her ass in the air as he stood up behind her.

It didn't take long for him to have her slightly raised off of her stomach with her ass posed in the doggy-style position. Quickly, he dropped his pants kicking them across the floor in a fury and lowered his boxers. Within seconds, he was sliding his stiff dick in and out of her wet pussy, fucking like his life depended on it. They fucked fast...hard, and moved all about the room.

Suddenly, G- Dolla pulled out, staring Shorty deep into her face, then tongue kissed her with passion. She held onto him tightly wishing he would say yes to her Atlanta plea. Before she knew it, he began to rub the tip of his dick on her pussy lips before stroking her again.

Damn, I'm in love, she told herself.

G-Dolla took long strokes as Shorty moaned like a porn star and threw that ass back at him. His eyes rolled to the back of head as he held onto her hips and punished her.

"Oh Shorty, damn! You feel so fuckin' good." he said.

"Lemme get on top," Shorty demanded.

Shorty slid herself off G-Dolla's love stick and turned around facing him face to face. He grabbed her ass roughly while she put her arms around his neck. She pushed her tongue in his mouth and flicked her tongue back and forth across his. G-Dolla then lifted her up by her ass, with her legs wrapped around his back and began to pound her insides.

"Ahhhhhhh!" Shorty screamed. She felt like she was going to burst.

"Damn, damn, yes, this is some good ass pussy!" G-Dolla groaned as he pounded Shorty's pussy back and forth on his dick.

With Shorty still in mid-air, G-Dolla walked back-wards where the back of his legs were touching the bed. He then sat on the bed and laid back. Shorty knew that this was her que to ride his dick like the bull at Cadillac Ranch. She rode it so well her has ass cheeks clapped against his stomach with force. G-Dolla grabbed her ass cheeks spreading them apart as Shorty pounced up and down on his enchanted 10-inch stick.

"Oh shit!" G-Dolla yelled as his toes started curling.

Still riding, Shorty sat up and gyrated her hips, looking deep into G-Dolla's eyes. She put her left hand on his chest and began rubbing on her clit with her right hand, still moving her hips in a circular motion.

"I'm about to cum! Ahhhhh!" G-Dolla screamed. Shorty picked up the pace of flicking her finger back and forth across her clit. Suddenly, Shorty started shaking as if she was having a seizure.

"I looooove you, Ahh Sh-iiii-ttt!" Shorty hollered as she collapsed on top of G-Dolla, trying to catch her breath.

"Damn, baby! What the hell were you trying to do to me?" he joked.

"Hahaha, you know you bring the freak out of me!" *Shorty, it's now or never*, she thought to herself. "Listen I have something to tell you that I think you should know," she said rolling onto to the bed.

"What?"

"No one broke into my house." She paused just long enough to give him the puppy dog eyes. "I'm at this hotel because I was dealing wit' a guy who's now working for the Feds. I'm caught up in some bullshit that I had nothing to do wit' so that's why I'm leaving to go to ATL," she explained sincerely.

G-Dolla's eyes ballooned "Who is this guy? I need to know so I can help you." He got up and put his boxers and pants back on.

"Sit back down," Shorty whined, "And where are you going?"

"Who is the guy?" he demanded, zipping his pants completely. He kept his puzzled expression.

"He isn't important. I've already taken care of his ass, so no need to worry about him," Shorty replied thinking that the duffle bag she gave Drape had enough evidence in it to seal his fate.

G-Dolla sat dumbfounded as he looked at Shorty shocked that she didn't want to tell him who the guy was. He felt so stupid for falling in love with someone so shiesty. In his heart he knew they could have had something great.

"Look, nigga, I really do love you, so are you gonna come wit' me, or what?"

G-Dolla seemed to look off into thin air. He couldn't bare to look into her lying eyes any longer. He knew her words were sincere and that she probably did really love him. But it would never work between them...not after what she had done. He just wanted to see how far she would continue lying. G-Dolla instantly had a flashback to when he took his Auntie to identify his cousin, Kim's body.

"Gary, do you hear me?" Shorty kept repeating. "What are you thinking about?" she asked lifting her body onto her knees.

"Shorty I really like you and started to fall in love with you, but you killed da wrong muthafucka! Ecstasy was my cousin!" G-Dolla shot back, never taking his eyes off Shorty.

He wanted to tell her how he found out that she was the person he'd dropped Ecstasy off to meet just before she was killed, but his gut wouldn't allow him to speak. It was the last outgoing call on his burn out cell phone that Ecstasy dialed when he dropped her off that gave away the killer. Shorty had murdered his loved one in cold blood and thought she was going to ride off into the sunset with her cousin. He eased his pistol out of his pants as he watched Shorty's mouth fall open in shock. She froze in fear as she saw the cold steel with a silencer in her lover's hand. Her heart skipped a beat as he cocked the hammer back.

"What are you doing?" she stammered rising off the bed, with a tear streaming down her face. "Don't do this, baby." Her eyes begged for mercy.

"When you lay down wit' dogs you get up wit' fleas,"

he taunted as he squeezed the trigger, hitting Shorty square in the chest. Her body fell back onto the bed as blood oozed from the center of her chest.

G-Dolla stood back wondering how he should've felt. He wasn't sure, but knew that his heart had been broken. With speed, he got dressed and looked around the room, making sure he had everything. His street smarts told him to wipe the room down leaving no prints. But his heart told him to leave the chain.

Quickly, he dug into his jean pocket and pulled out the necklace with the cross that his mother had left him. It was supposedly a gift he'd planned on giving Shorty. Quickly, he threw the chain over her body, grabbing the bag of money off the floor. Shorty laid in shock, eyes wide open, laid flat on her back, gasping for air. He couldn't stand by any longer to watch her die. He left swiftly thinking she'd betrayed him and played him for his love.

SNITCH

CHAPTER 37

ONE MONTH LATER

Drape knew at this point he had nothing to lose. His ten-year sentence was already etched in stone. He was being charged with Ecstasy's murder and the three bricks the Feds found on him. Even though the murder weapon was found in his trunk with his fingerprints on it, Mr. Goldstein informed Drape he had nothing to lose if he took it to trial. However, his lawyer then explained to him that he had a good chance claiming self-defense for shooting Tim. It was amazing how even after sustaining a shot to his abdomen, Tim still managed to survive. He was recovering at the hospital, but still faced charges on his own.

While sitting in the Federal Detention Center without bond, Drape heard about Angel's death through word of mouth from different niggas passing through. This confirmed what Detective Burns had said. When he heard the news, he tried to call home and speak to his mom, but she wouldn't accept any of his calls. His mother even refused to come see to him, especially since she blamed him for Angel's death.

Drape was emotionally hurt over the loss of his brother. They were close and his heart ached every time he thought about Angel. His mother obviously didn't understand that Drape tried his best to save Angel, but things just didn't work out the way he'd planned. While she grieved, Drape didn't know how to comfort her at a time like this, so he decided to give her space, hoping one day that she'd come around.

"Lopez you have a visit!" the correctional officer yelled.

Drape hadn't heard from anyone or received a visit since he was arrested. At one point his life was full of family and people who looked out for his well being. Now, everyone in his corner had turned their backs...even Diona. They were on terrible terms. She was bitter not only because he'd gotten locked up once again, but because he'd missed the birth of their daughter. He had constantly tried to get in touch with her, but she refused his collect calls. Drape got off his steel bunk and put on his oversized orange jumpsuit and brown flip-flops. He then headed up to the visiting booth. He figured it was his lawyer because he was the only person he had at this point, win or lose.

Drape was shocked when he saw Diona sitting in the visiting booth as he approached. She barely recognized him because his clean cut shaven face was now a bushy beard and his low cut fade was now a curly afro. To make matters worse, the stress he was under had caused him to lose a tremendous amount of weight.

As he looked at her, she was still pretty as ever instantly making him yearn to touch her. He felt completely helpless. His heart began to throb looking at the woman he had every intention of making his wife. He'd even bought her a platinum 4-carat princess cut diamond ring before his last meeting with Agent Lewis at the coffee shop. With him never getting the opportunity to give it to her, Drape knew she would never truly understand how sorry he felt.

"Hey," Drape said. "I'm so glad you here."

"Look, I'm only here because I have something to

show you," Diona mumbled as she reached down beside her and lifted up a baby carrier sitting it on the booth counter.

Drape stood up and placed his face against the glass and started to cry as he admired the beautiful, caramel skin, curly headed little girl who slept peacefully in her cute pink outfit.

"Mami, she's beautiful. What's her name?"

"Karma," Diona said looking Drape directly in his eyes. She could see the pain he felt, but had no remorse. She'd never looked at him this way before. It was like the purity from her heart was gone. "I came to give you your first and last look at our daughter. It's a shame you're going to miss out on her life," she continued.

"Diona, I'm sorry. I love you with all of my heart and I've made mistakes. Please don't do this to me. I want and need my daughter in my life. I'm sorry for everything and...," he pleaded but before he could finish, Diona cut him off.

"Whatever. You can save that shit because I'm not trying to hear it. Oh, I heard your bitch Shorty got shot and survived. Missed her heart by inches, so you should be happy. Maybe once she recover's she'll come see your ass." When Drake's eyes widened Diona continued. "Drape, or should I say Ce'sar? Considering you're not draped in anything these days. There will never be you and me again. We have no dealings period, point blank. You think fucking Shorty and other hoes was the last straw. Don't even deny it because it's written all over your face. I told you before that we would all suffer, but you didn't listen. Now, it's too late. Don't you want better for yourself and our daughter? I guess not, you selfish asshole. No sirves para nada, which means you're good for nothing," she said in a nasty tone.

"Damn! Who taught you to talk like dat?"

"I learned from the best!" Diona replied then hung up the phone. She then grabbed their daughter and walked off.

He stared at her as she left knowing this would truly be his first and last time seeing them. She kept walking never looking back. He thought to himself that she was the only woman he ever truly loved and it angered him that he'd risked her and his daughter for some bullshit. He knew he'd made her heart turn cold. She wasn't the same anymore. Even though it wasn't official, Diona would always be wifey to him and Drape was willing to wait until she forgave him. He hoped the love Diona still had for him would make her have a change of heart.

Drape hurried back to his cell that had a clear view of the parking lot, two stories down. He peered down into the lot at Diona as she struggled carrying his daughter in the car seat. As she walked, a silver Jaguar pulled up and stopped. Moments later, a big burly man got out of the driver's seat and approached the rear door opening it so Diona could place their daughter inside. After the two got back into the car and drove off, Drape's stomach dropped as he caught sight of the license plates, which read "INVESTOR."

A Message From The Publisher

Are you ready for a change?

Once again, thank you for allowing Life Changing Books (LCB) into your mind and your hearts. Let me start by saying, this book should have both entertained you and made you take a life changing look into the mirror. Yes, it's fiction but it touches on familiar paths that either you've taken, someone you know has explored, or a road that is totally foreign and still has you drooling at the mouth.

I'm positive there was a character that made you laugh, cry, and sometimes shout, "Are there really people like this in the world?" Unfortunately, the answer is yes. They have major flaws just as I do.

Let's make a change!

Like so many of you I have goals and aspirations as a publisher: My heartfelt goal is to publish works that include events and characters that resonate in you in such a way that when the last page is turned you find yourself asking, "What can I do to help make this world a better place?" So, I ask, what are your goals and aspirations? How can you improve yourself and your community? It all begins with you...one simple move.

I encourage you to take a step beyond what you have read and put a plan into action. Get involved in your community. Become a mentor. Re-create your goals. Is it that you want to improve a new relationship with someone you care about? Thought about going back to school? What about writing a book? If so, reach out to us at 301-362-6508 we can tell you how to get started. Or do you simply have a desire to do something good for someone else?

Make the change!

I am.
We are.
Life Changing Books.
Thank you for your support!

Azarel
CEO/Publisher

LCB BOOK TITLES

The Dirty Divorce
A NOVEL BY
MISS KP

My Man, Her Son
A Novel
J. Tremble

CHEDDA BOYZ
A NOVEL BY C.J. HUDSON

LOVE HEIST
A novel by Jackie D

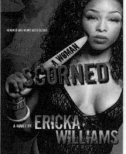

A WOMAN SCORNED
A NOVEL BY ERICKA WILLIAMS

Millionaire Mistress 3
CHLOE'S REVENGE
By Tyhani

CARBON COPY
AZAREL

GOOD GIRL Gone BAD
DANETTE MAJETTE

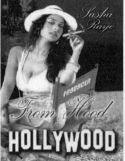

Sasha Raye
From Hood 2 HOLLYWOOD

See More Titles At

www.lifechangingbooks.net

IN STORES NOW

COMING SOON

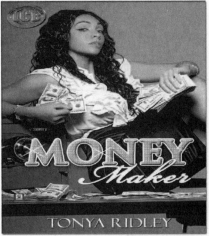

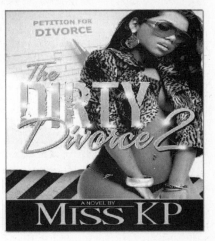

FOR MORE TITLES
LOG ONTO
www.lifechangingbooks.net

ORDER FORM

MAIL TO:
PO Box 423
Brandywine, MD 20613
301-362-6508

FAX TO:
301-856-4116

Ship to: _____
Address: _____

Date: _____ Phone: _____

Email: _____

City & State: _____ Zip: _____

Make all money orders and cashiers checks payable to: **Life Changing Books**

Qty.	ISBN	Title	Release Date	Price
	0-9741394-5-9	Nothin Personal by Tyrone Wallace	Jul-06	$ 15.00
	0-9741394-2-4	Bruised by Azarel	Jul-05	$ 15.00
	0-9741394-7-5	Bruised 2: The Ultimate Revenge by Azarel	Oct-06	$ 15.00
	0-9741394-3-2	Secrets of a Housewife by J. Tremble	Feb-06	$ 15.00
	0-9724003-5-4	I Shoulda Seen It Comin by Danette Majette	Jan-06	$ 15.00
	0-9741394-4-0	The Take Over by Tonya Ridley	Apr-06	$ 15.00
	0-9741394-6-7	The Millionaire Mistress by Tiphani	Nov-06	$ 15.00
	1-934230-99-5	More Secrets More Lies by J. Tremble	Feb-07	$ 15.00
	1-934230-98-7	Young Assassin by Mike G.	Mar-07	$ 15.00
	1-934230-95-2	A Private Affair by Mike Warren	May-07	$ 15.00
	1-934230-94-4	All That Glitters by Ericka M. Williams	Jul-07	$ 15.00
	1-934230-93-6	Deep by Danette Majette	Jul-07	$ 15.00
	1-934230-96-0	Flexin & Sexin Volume 1	Jun-07	$ 15.00
	1-934230-92-8	Talk of the Town by Tonya Ridley	Jul-07	$ 15.00
	1-934230-89-8	Still a Mistress by Tiphani	Nov-07	$ 15.00
	1-934230-91-X	Daddy's House by Azarel	Nov-07	$ 15.00
	1-934230-87-1-	Reign of a Hustler by Nissa A. Showell	Jan-08	$ 15.00
	1-934230-86-3	Something He Can Feel by Marissa Montelih	Feb-08	$ 15.00
	1-934230-88-X	Naughty Little Angel by J. Tremble	Feb-08	$ 15.00
	1-934230847	In Those Jeans by Chantel Jolie	Jun-08	$ 15.00
	1-934230855	Marked by Capone	Jul-08	$ 15.00
	1-934230820	Rich Girls by Kendall Banks	Oct-08	$ 15.00
	1-934230839	Expensive Taste by Tiphani	Nov-08	$ 15.00
	1-934230782	Brooklyn Brothel by C. Stecko	Jan-09	$ 15.00
	1-934230669	Good Girl Gone bad by Danette Majette	Mar-09	$ 15.00
	1-934230804	From Hood to Hollywood by Sasha Raye	Mar-09	$ 15.00
	1-934230707	Sweet Swagger by Mike Warren	Jun-09	$ 15.00
	1-934230677	Carbon Copy by Azarel	Jul-09	$ 15.00
	1-934230723	Millionaire Mistress 3 by Tiphani	Nov-09	$ 15.00
	1-934230715	A Woman Scorned by Ericka Williams	Nov-09	$ 15.00
	1-934230685	My Man Her Son by J. Tremble	Feb-10	$ 15.00
	1-924230731	Love Heist by Jackie D.	Mar-10	$ 15.00
	1-934230812	Flexin & Sexin Volume 2	Apr-10	$ 15.00
	1-934230748	The Dirty Divorce by Miss KP	May-10	$ 15.00
			Total for Books	$

* Prison Orders- Please allow up to three (3) weeks for delivery.

Please Note: We are not held responsible for returned prison orders. Make sure the facility will receive books before ordering.

Shipping Charges (add $4.25 for 1-4 books*) $

Total Enclosed (add lines) $

*Shipping and Handling of 5-10 books is $6.25, please contact us if your order is more than 10 books.
(301)362-6508